Disney
PLANES
FIRE & RESCUE

HEROES OF THE SKY

By Frank Berrios
Illustrated by the Disney Storybook Art Team

A GOLDEN BOOK • NEW YORK

ISBN 978-0-7364-3231-3
randomhouse.com/kids
Printed in the United States of America
10 9 8 7 6 5 4 3 2 1

Dusty Crophopper is in the lead. He is a racing champion!

Sparky and Chug are Dusty's biggest fans.

Dusty will be performing at Propwash Junction's
upcoming Corn Festival.

Barbara and Brody are excited about all the tourists who will stay at their motel during the Corn Festival.

Skipper and Dusty fly high above Propwash Junction.

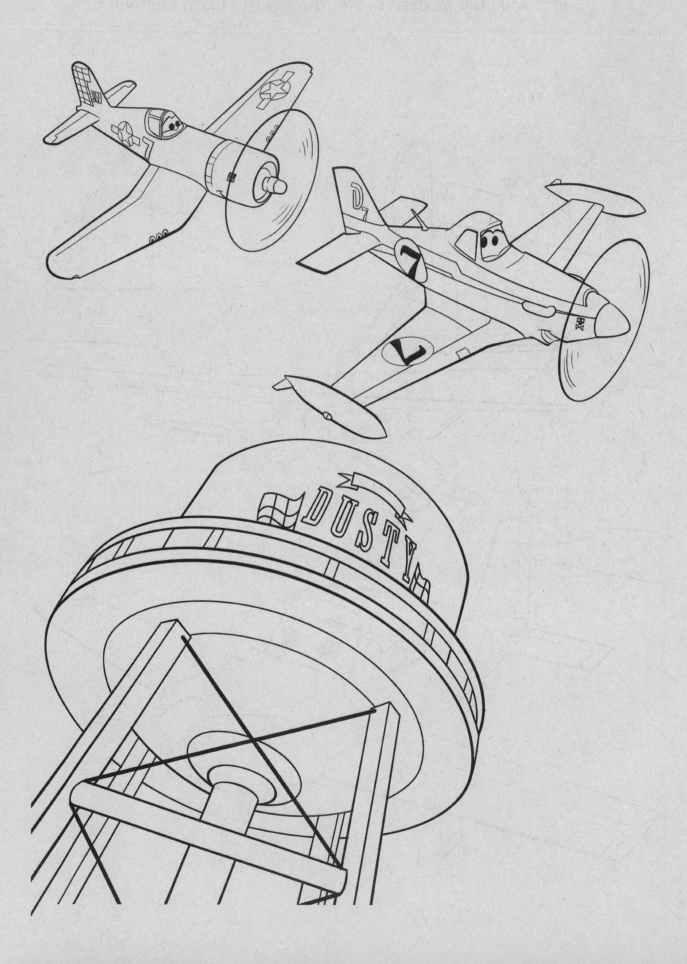

Color this poster of Skipper and Dusty to hang on your wall!

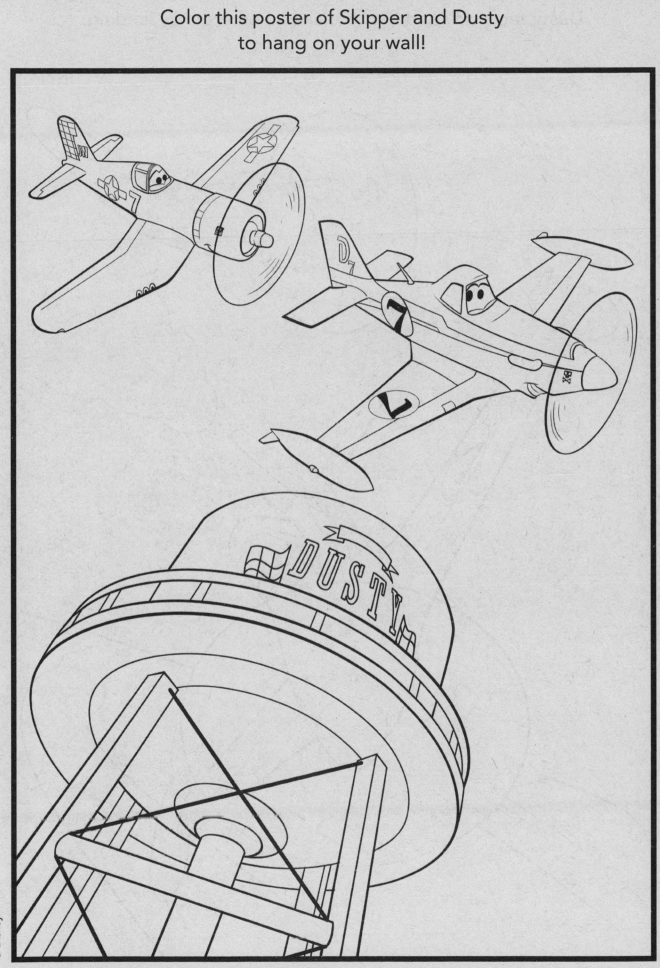

Dusty feels sick and has to make an emergency landing.

Dusty's mechanic, Dottie, does some tests
to see what is wrong with Dusty.

Dottie tells Dusty that his gearbox is broken,
and that he can no longer race.

Dusty is really upset that he can no longer race.
Skipper tries to cheer him up.

Dusty's old boss, Leadbottom, hopes Dusty will return to crop dusting.

Dusty wants to prove that he can still race.
But Dusty is so distracted that he loses control!

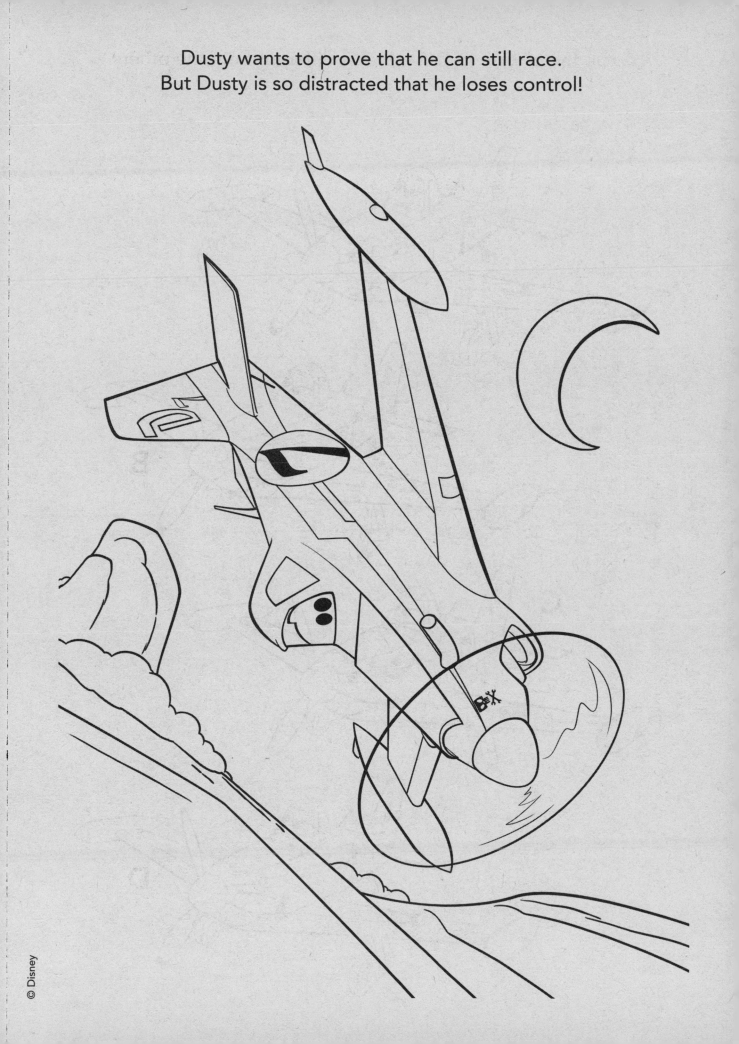

Circle the picture of Dusty that is different from the others.

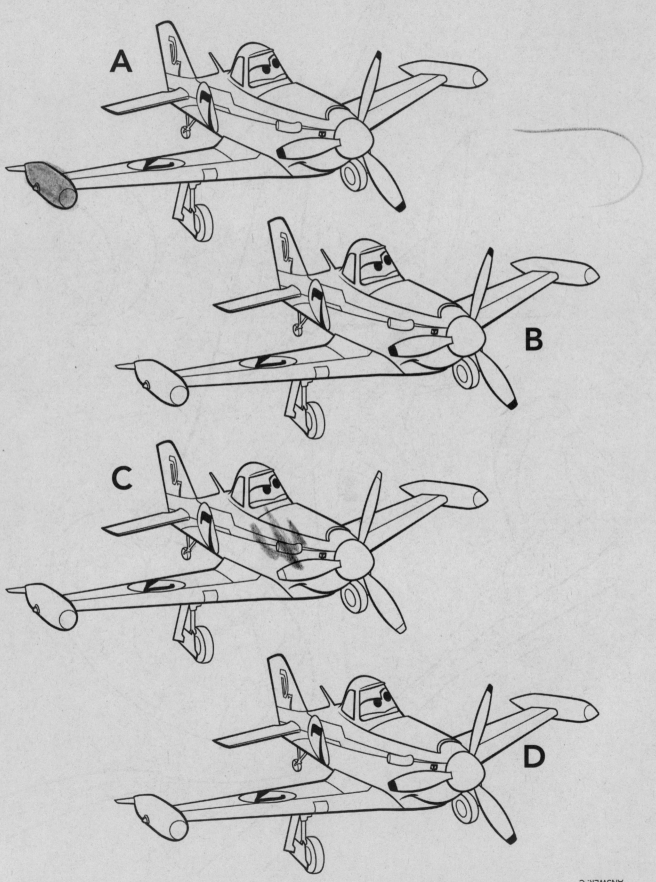

A

B

C

D

Dusty crashes into a gas pump at the Fill 'n' Fly,
the local service station.

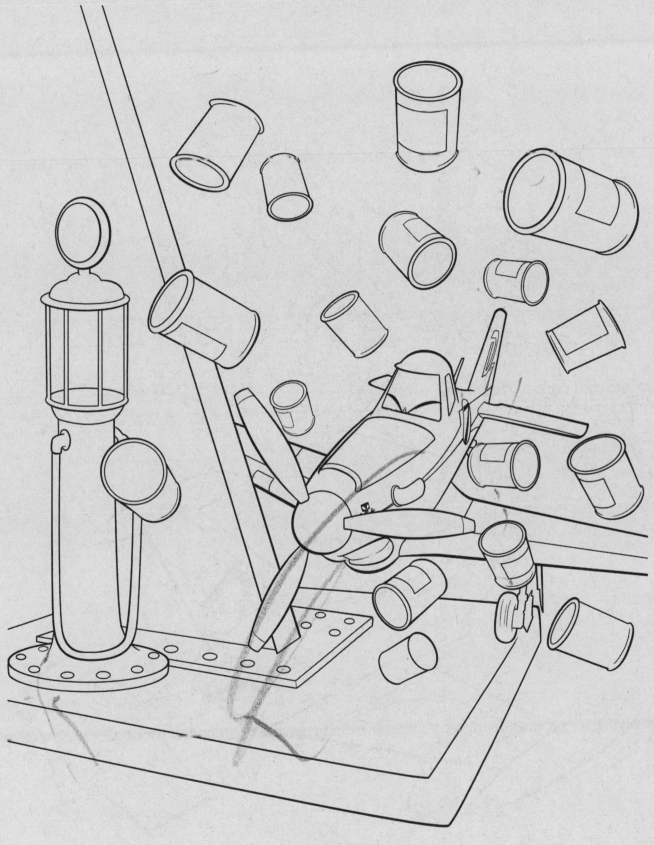

A huge fire erupts at the Fill 'n' Fly!

Propwash Junction's old fire engine tries to put out the fire, but there are too many leaks in his fire hose.

To learn the name of this fire engine, cross out every *T*.
Then write the remaining letters in order on the blanks.

TMTTATYTTDTATYT

__ _ _ _ _ _ __

Mayday and Dusty tip over the town's water tower
to put out the big fire.

Until Mayday gets new fire-fighting gear and the town finds a second firefighter, Propwash Junction's runway is shut down!

Everyone in Propwash Junction is upset.
Without an open runway, the Corn Festival will be canceled!

Dusty volunteers to train to become
Propwash Junction's second firefighter.

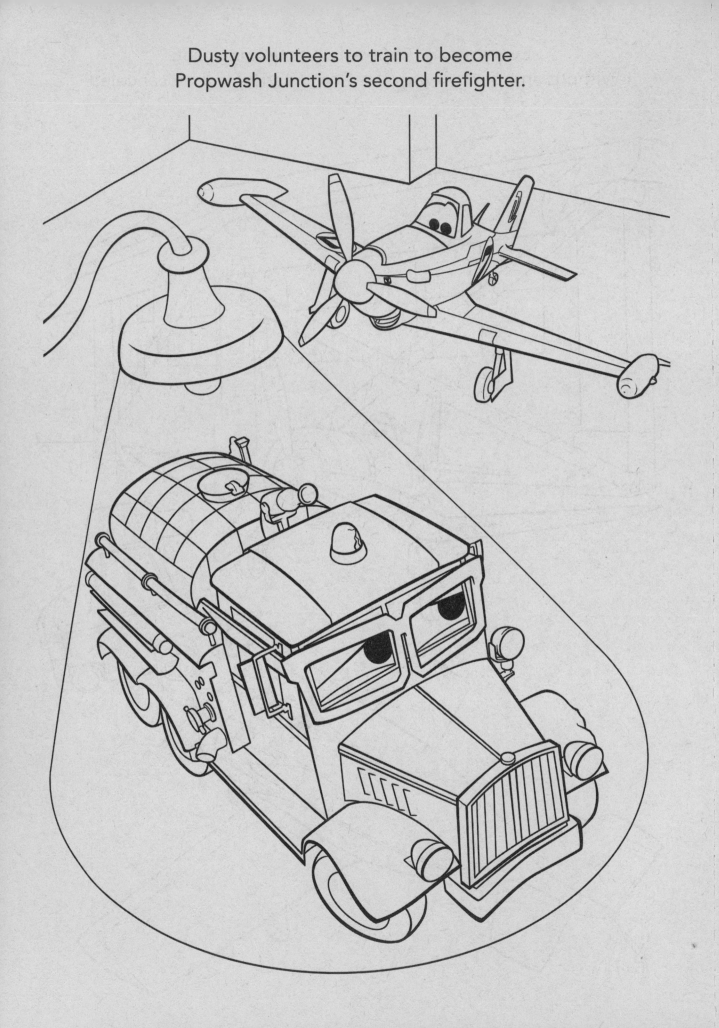

Chug makes sure all of the tractors have crossed the road before Dusty takes off.

Mayday and Dottie wish Dusty luck as he leaves for his firefighter training.

Dusty flies to Piston Peak National Park.

Count the deer on this page. How many are there?

Dusty zooms through a giant old tree.

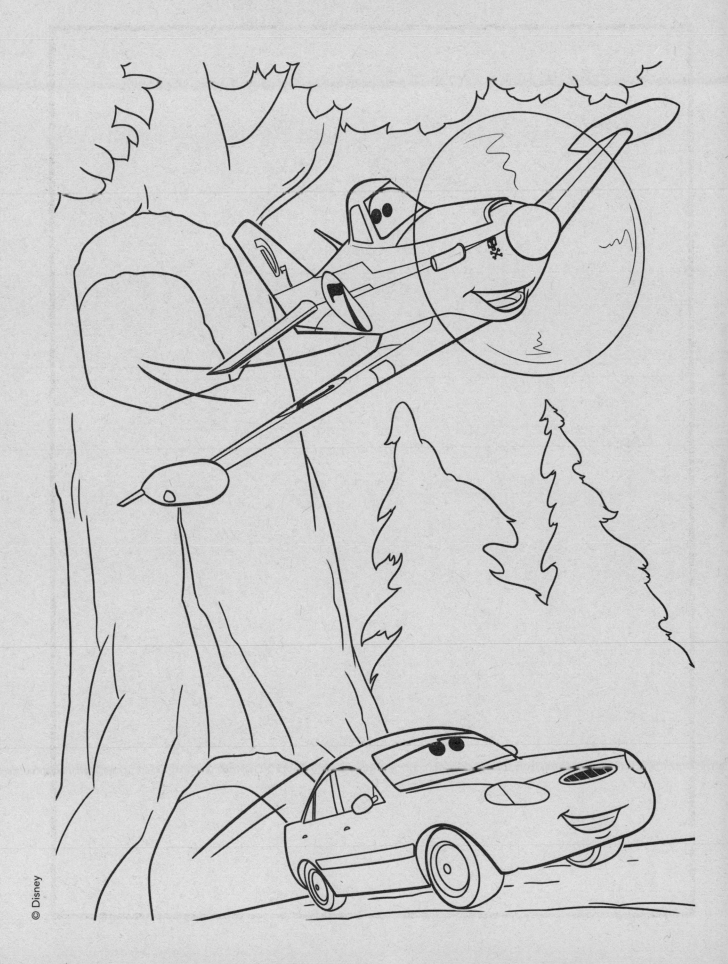

Use your stickers to create a Planes poster to hang on your wall!

Winnie and Harvey are visiting Piston Peak National Park
to find the spot where they shared their first kiss.

Circle the shadow that belongs to Winnie.

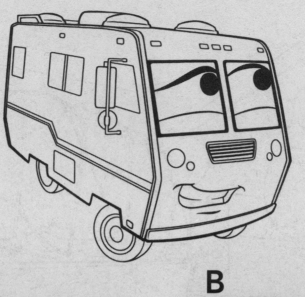

A

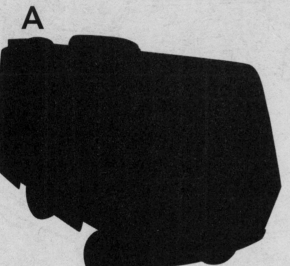

B

C

D

Cad Spinner is Park Superintendent. He runs the Fusel Lodge with the help of André the concierge.

Patch watches for fires from the control tower
at Piston Peak's Air Base.

Windlifter, a heavy-lift helicopter, is part of
the Piston Peak Air Attack Team.

Color this poster of Windlifter to hang on your wall!

When Lil' Dipper, a super-scooper, isn't putting out fires,
she likes to sun herself.

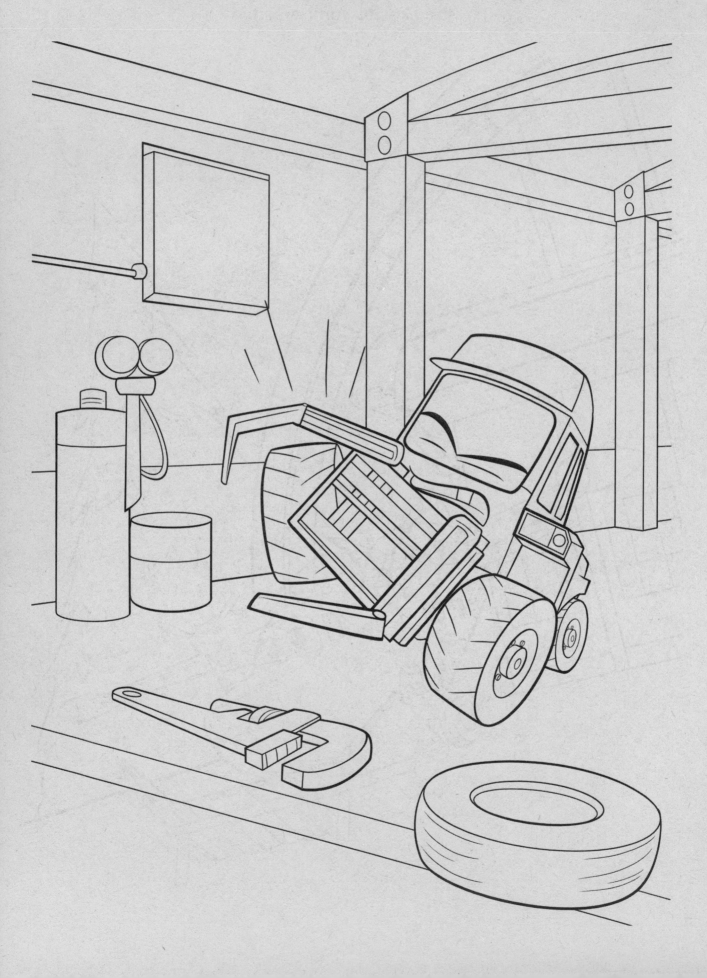

Cabbie, a massive transport plane,
carries the smokejumpers to the fires.

Drip is a smokejumper—and a daredevil.
He almost lands on Dusty during one of his stunts!

Dynamite is the leader of the smokejumpers.

Circle the picture of Dynamite that is different.

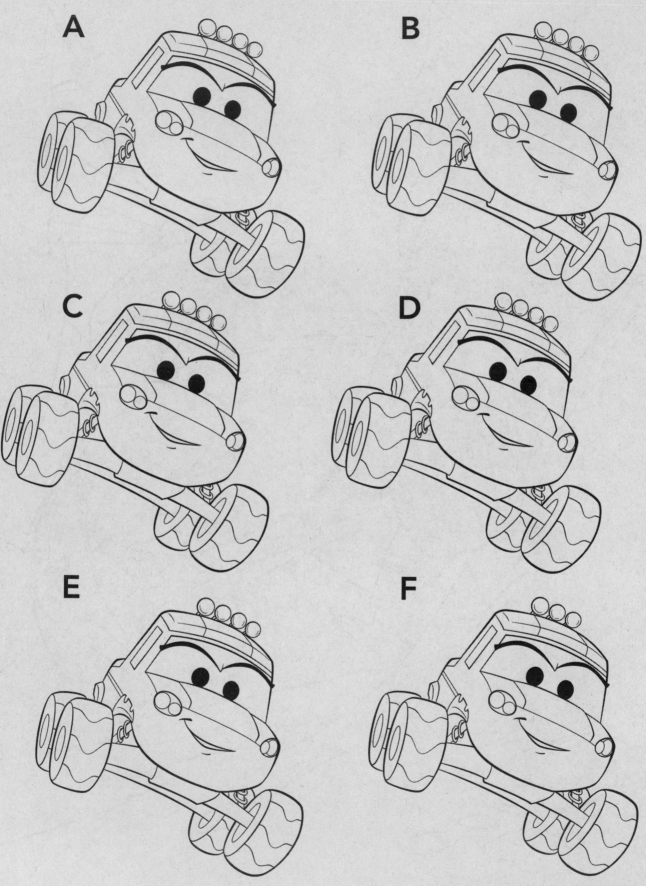

A B C D E F

Pinecone, Avalanche, and Blackout are smokejumpers.
They use parachutes to float down to fight fires on the ground.

Solve the maze to help Pinecone, Avalanche, and Blackout find Dynamite.

START

FINISH

Blade Ranger is the leader of the Piston Peak Air Attack Team.

Color this poster of Blade to hang on your bedroom door!

Dipper drops fire retardant to put out the blaze below.

Maru hoses Dusty off after a fire.

Dipper tries to explain to Blade that Dusty is a famous racer,
but Blade is not impressed.

Maru gives Dusty pontoons, but Dusty has
a hard time getting used to them.

Dipper teaches Dusty how to scoop water with his pontoons.

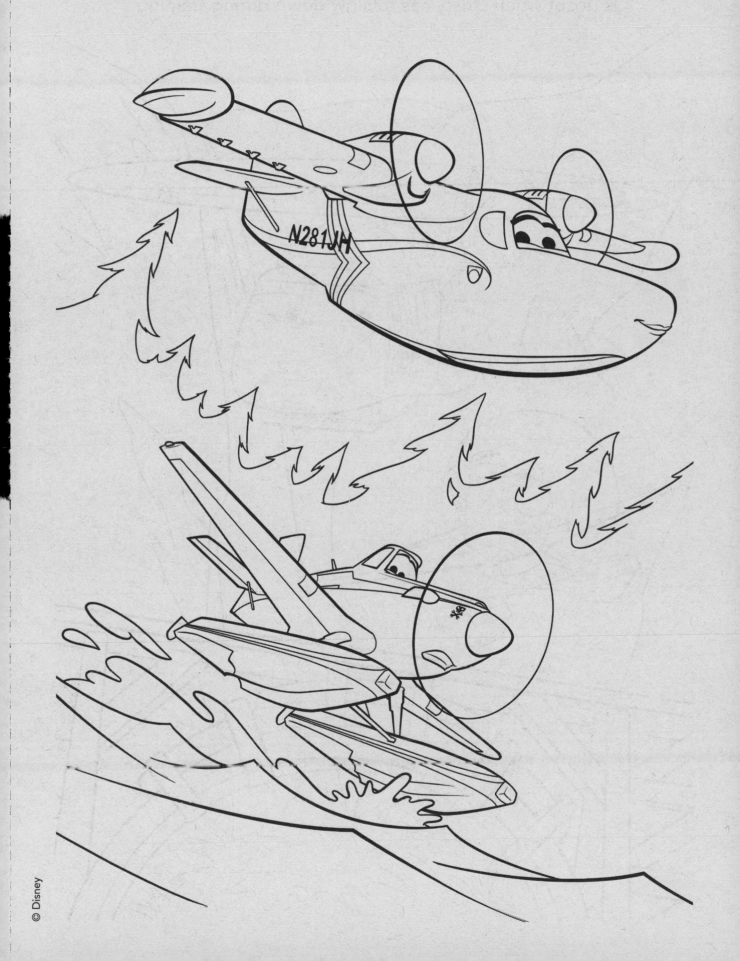

Blade doesn't know about Dusty's damaged gearbox and is upset when Dusty has to slow down during training.

Dusty is surprised to find Dipper watching him when he tries to get some sleep.

Dusty practices dropping fire retardant on flaming barrels.

Dusty mistakes a campfire for a real wildfire—
and drops fire retardant on some very unhappy campers.

Chug and Sparky radio Dusty with good news—
they found a new gearbox for him!

Cad Spinner is rude. He talks on his cell phone all the time.

Maru, Dusty, and Dipper watch an episode of an old TV show called *CHoPs* that Blade used to star in.

Blade scouts for spot fires during a lightning storm.

Blackout uses his saw to cut down trees in the line of fire.

Avalanche bulldozes debris from a clearing
so there won't be any fuel left for the fire.

Drip uses his grabber-claw to clear logs away from the fire.

Pinecone uses her rake to remove
small logs and debris from the line of fire.

Dusty swoops in at the last moment to drop retardant
on the fire surrounding the smokejumpers!

Dusty and Dipper visit the Fusel Lodge, where Dipper almost knocks down an ice sculpture!

Pulaski is the Fusel Lodge's massive structural fire engine.

Circle the shadow that belongs to Pulaski.

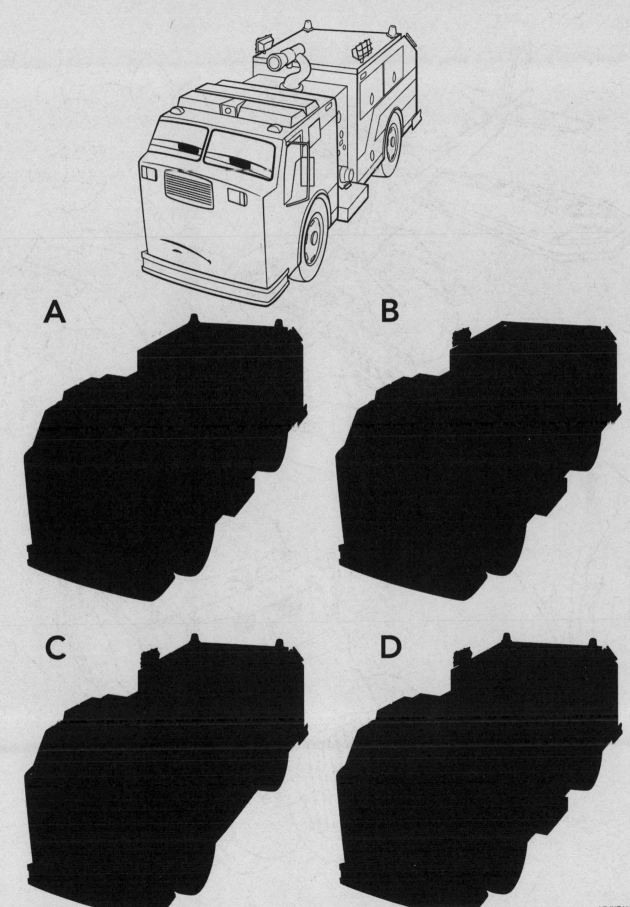

A

B

C

D

Ol' Jammer has been a ranger at
Piston Peak National Park for seventy-two years!

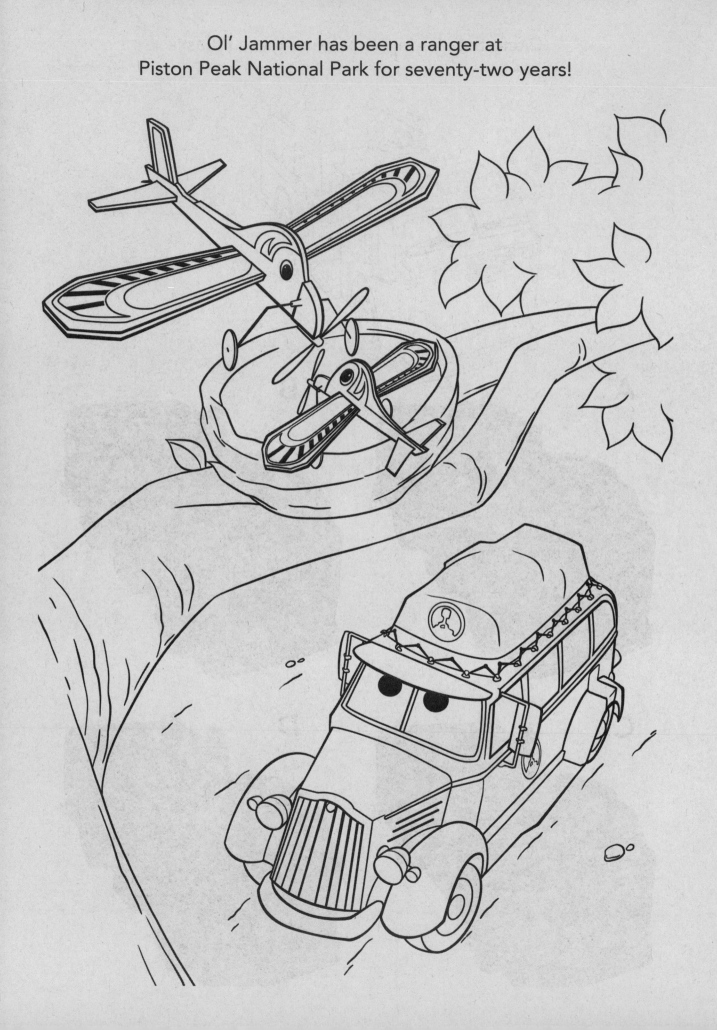

The Secretary of the Interior of the United States
is visiting Piston Peak National Park.

Dusty receives horrible news from his friends back in Propwash Junction: they haven't been able to find him a new gearbox after all.

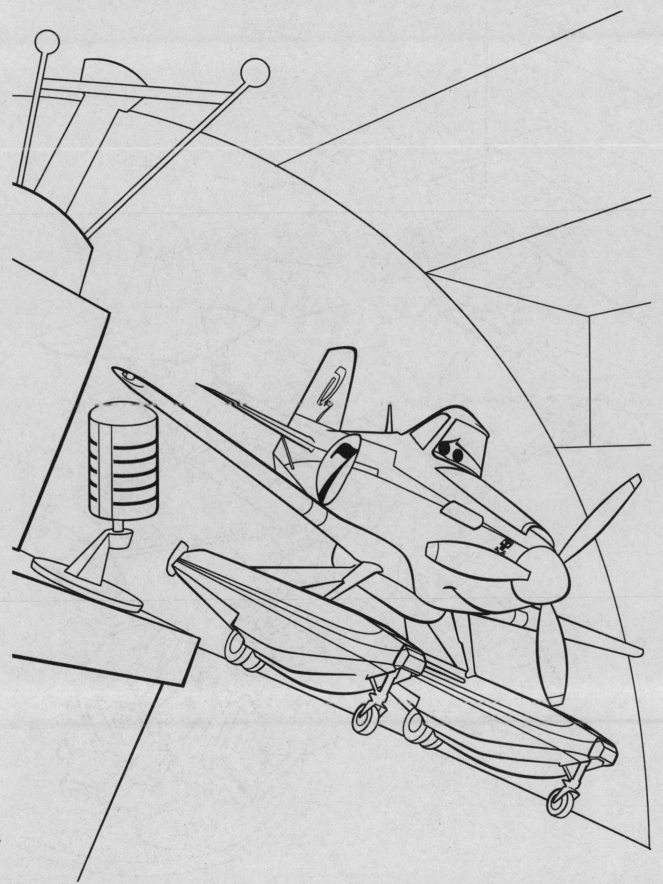

The klaxon blares as Maru loads up Dipper with
a fresh batch of fire retardant.

Dusty is too distracted to listen to Blade's instructions.

Blade is upset with Dusty for not following orders.

Circle the shadow that belongs to Blade.

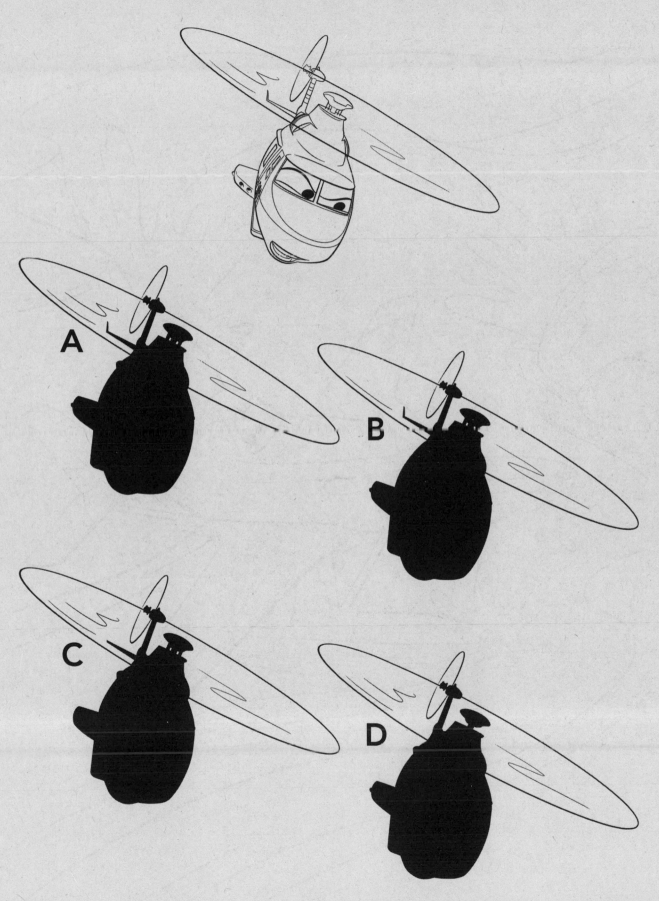

ANSWER: A.

Dusty gets stuck in the rapids as he tries to scoop water.

Solve the maze to help Blade find Dusty.

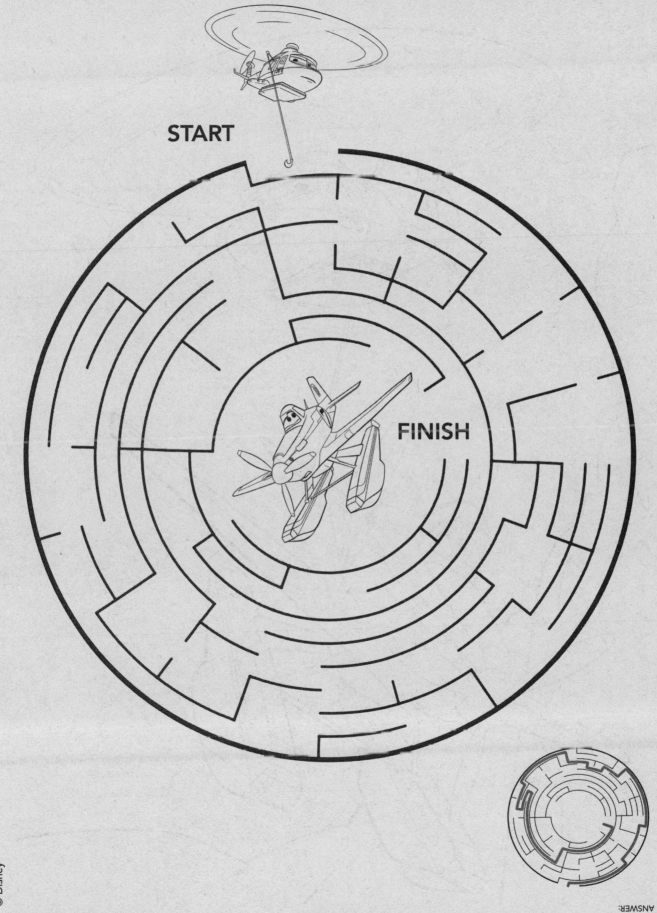

START

FINISH

ANSWER:

Blade rescues Dusty just before he goes over a waterfall!

Pulaski orders Cad to evacuate the Fusel Lodge's guests,
but Cad doesn't listen.

Cad is too distracted by the grand reopening
of the Fusel Lodge to notice the fire.

Pulaski helps the guests evacuate the Fusel Lodge.

To escape the fire, Blade and Dusty
hunker down in an old mine shaft.

The heat of the fire damages Blade's engine,
and he crashes after trying to take off.

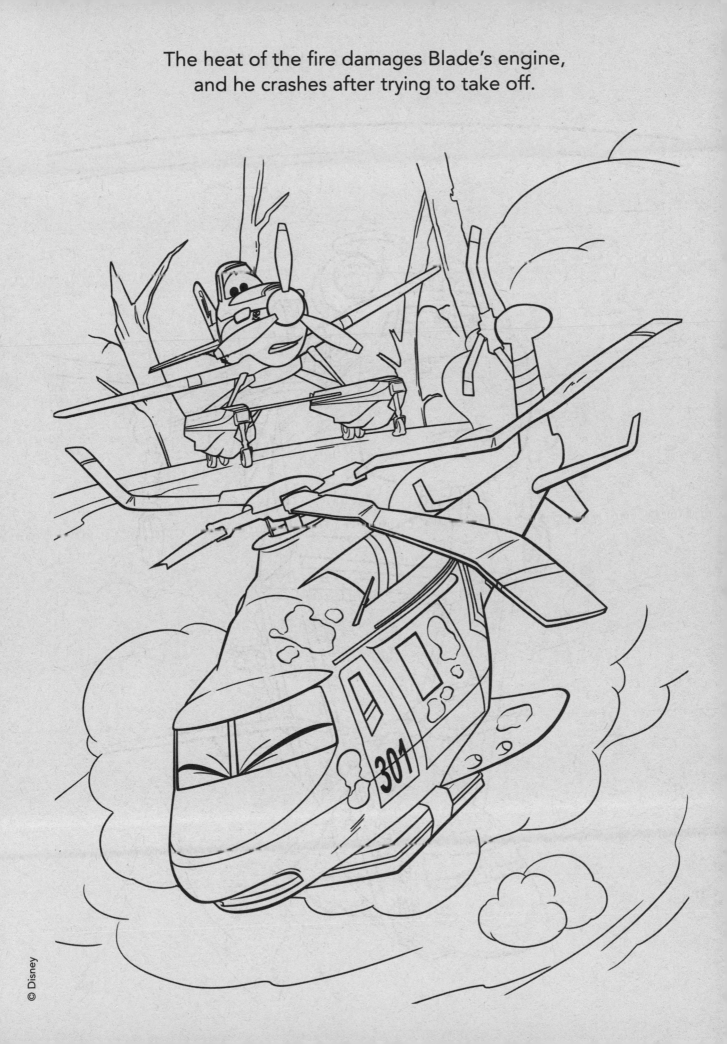

Windlifter carries Blade back to base.

Maru explains to Dusty that Blade is going to be okay.

Pulaski fights the fire while Ol' Jammer
helps the guests evacuate the park.

Cad Spinner is selfish. He reroutes all of the water
in the park to the Fusel Lodge.

Dusty learns that Blade became a firefighter after his former costar, Nick "Loop'n'" Lopez, crashed one day while on set.

Guests visiting Piston Peak are anxious to leave
the park to escape the fire.

Because of the fire, the Piston Peak Railway train
is unable to leave the park.

Maru can't give the firefighters water because Cad rerouted it all to the Fusel Lodge.

Dipper and Dusty have to fly through the fire to get to the guests.

Dusty drops fire retardant on the flames so the train
can leave the park.

The smokejumpers work to clear the road so all
of the guests can evacuate.

Harvey and Winnie are trapped on
an old wooden bridge surrounded by fire.

Dusty flies as fast as he can to rescue Harvey and Winnie.

Blade swoops in and uses his hoist to keep
Harvey and Winnie from falling off the bridge.

Dusty flies up the face of the waterfall
to scoop water to put out the fire.

Dusty puts out the fire just in time to save Harvey and Winnie!

Harvey and Winnie are happy to be out of danger.

Blade is proud of Dusty, but Dusty has pushed himself too hard.

Dusty's engine fails and he crashes into the trees!

Maru tells Dusty that he was able to fix Dusty's gearbox.
Now Dusty can be a racer *and* a firefighter!

Blade tells Dusty that he has earned his certification.
It is time to fly home to Propwash Junction!

Solve the maze to help Dusty return to Propwash Junction.

START

FINISH

Propwash Junction's runway is officially reopened!

The new and improved Propwash Junction Fire Department
has never looked better.

Chug and Sparky enjoy the Corn Festival.

Leadbottom wins first prize for his Vita-minamulch at the Corn Festival.

Kate is the biggest fan of the Corn Festival.
She even has a corncob costume!

Cad Spinner was relocated to Death Valley.

Dusty and the Piston Peak Air Attack Team
put on a show for everyone at the Corn Festival.

Color this poster to hang on your wall!

Yay, Dusty!

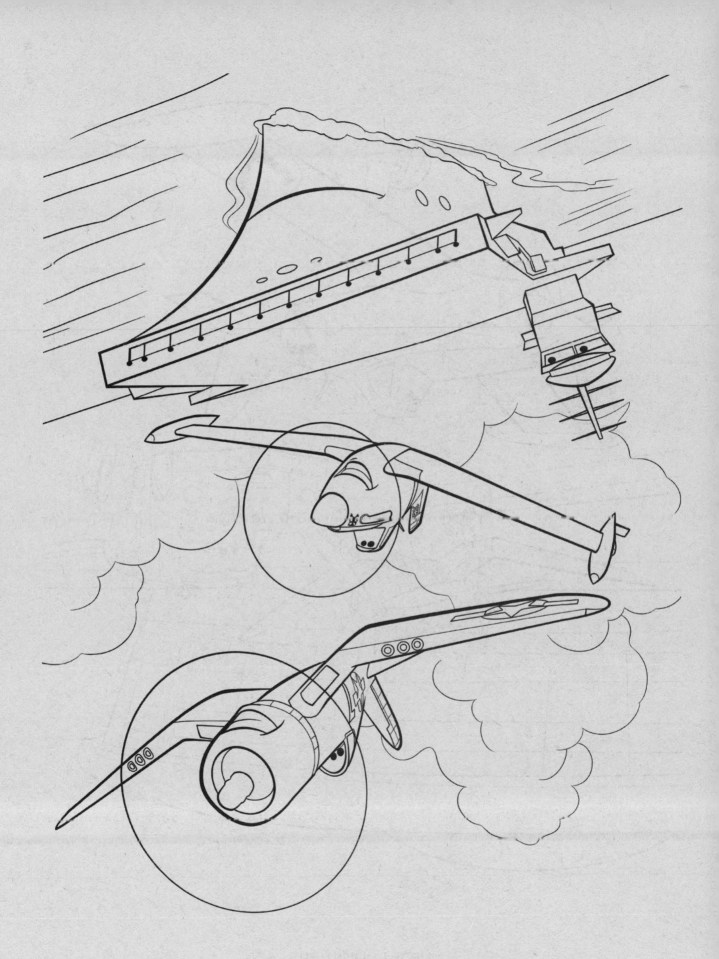

Dusty and Skipper are high-flying friends!

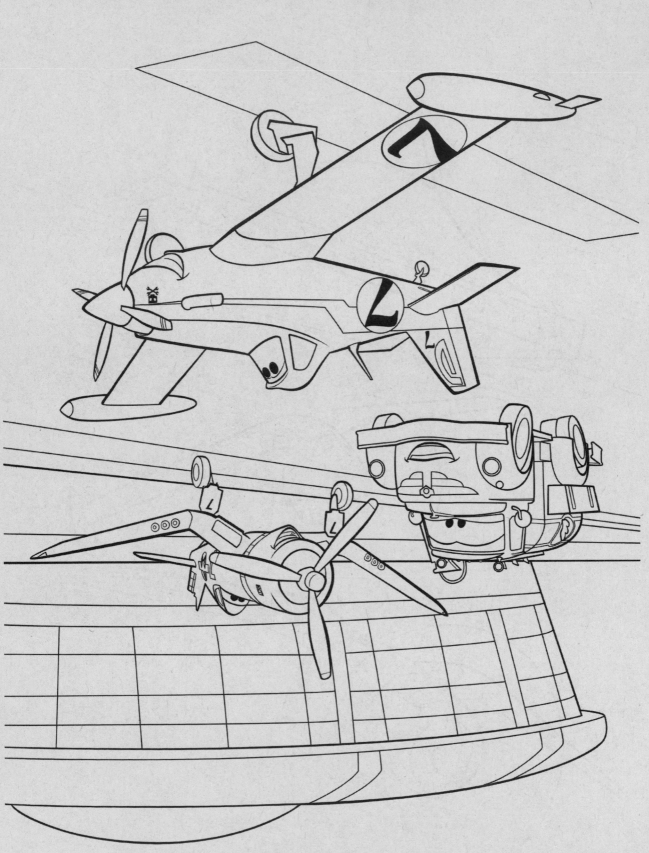

With the help of his friends, Dusty has become a high-flying
champion racer!

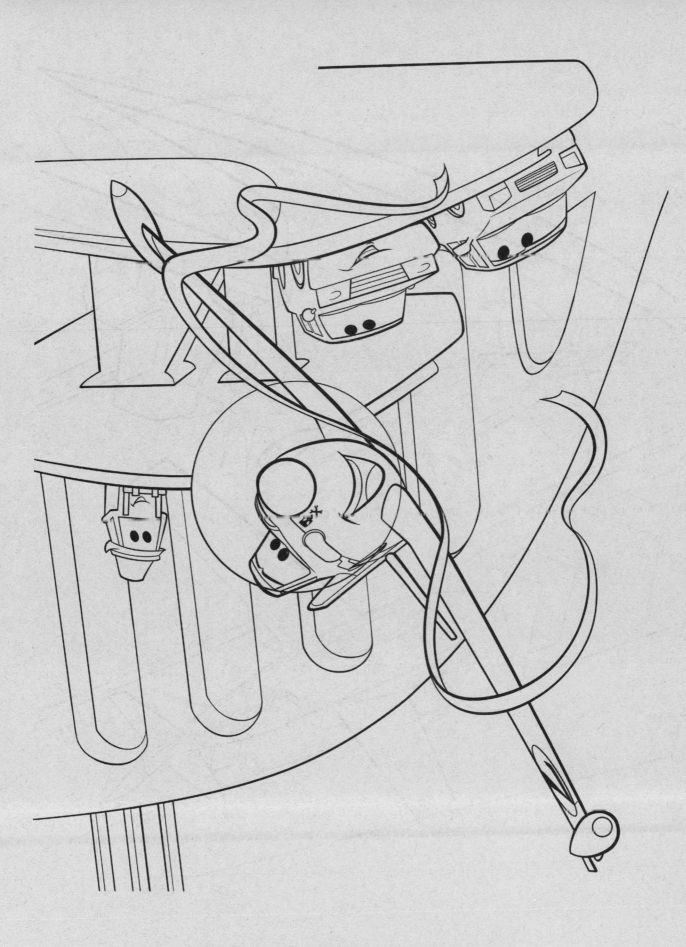

ZOOM! Dusty blazes across the finish line first—and wins
the Wings Around The Globe Rally!

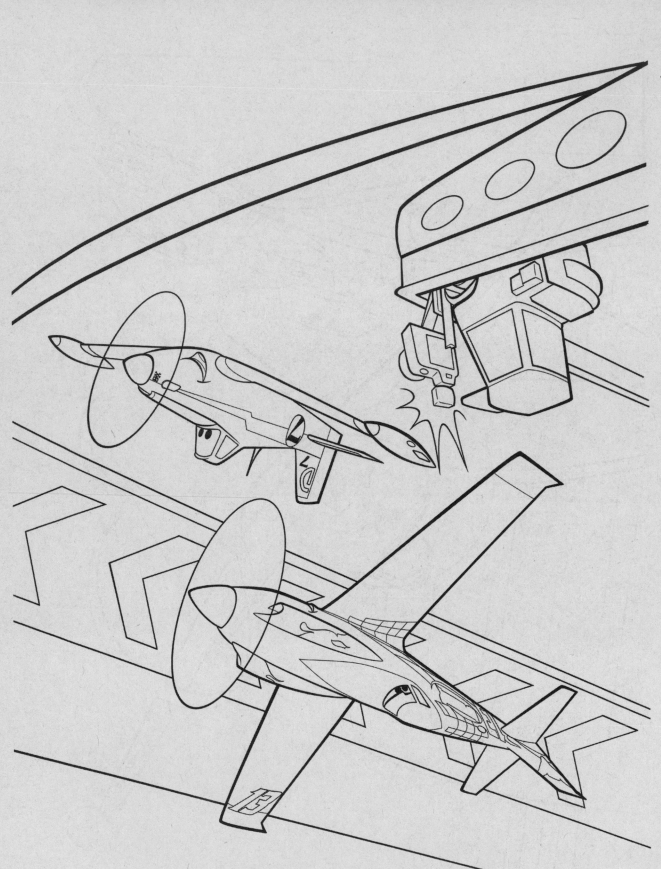

Ripslinger smiles and poses for the cameras.
He thinks he has won the race.

Solve the maze and help Dusty catch up with Ripslinger.

START

FINISH

Dusty finally faces his fear of heights! Up in the tailwinds, he flies
faster than ever before!

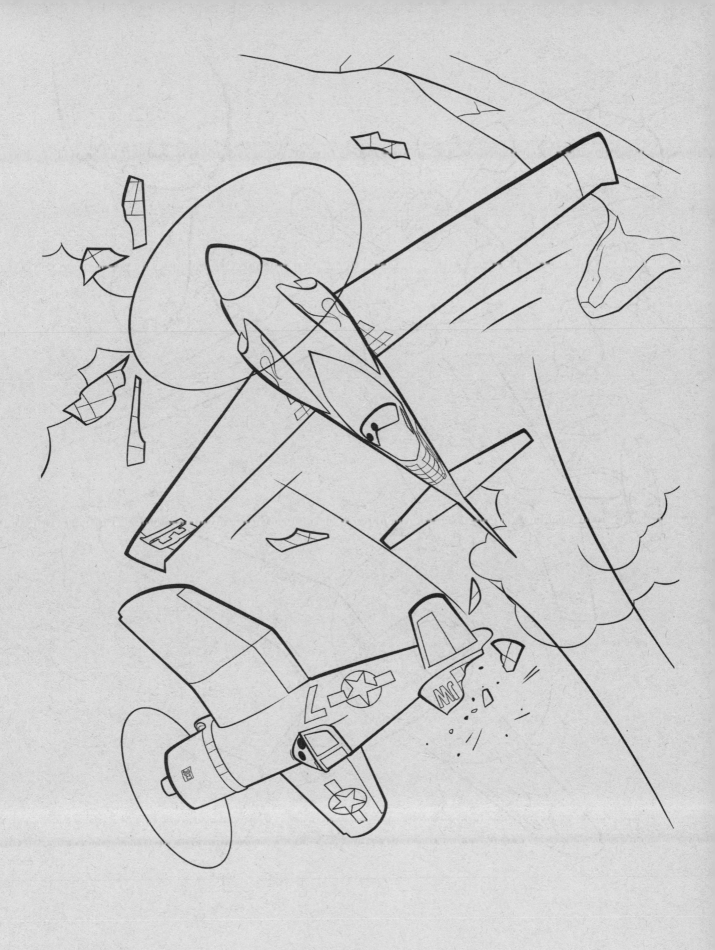

Ripslinger crashes into Skipper—he'll do whatever it takes
to win the race!

Skipper faces his fear of flying—and saves Dusty from Ned and Zed!

The final leg of the race begins! Dusty is off to a good start until
Ned and Zed try to make him crash!

EMERGENCY

Dottie helps Dusty get ready to race!

Help Dusty find the path that will lead to his new parts.

START

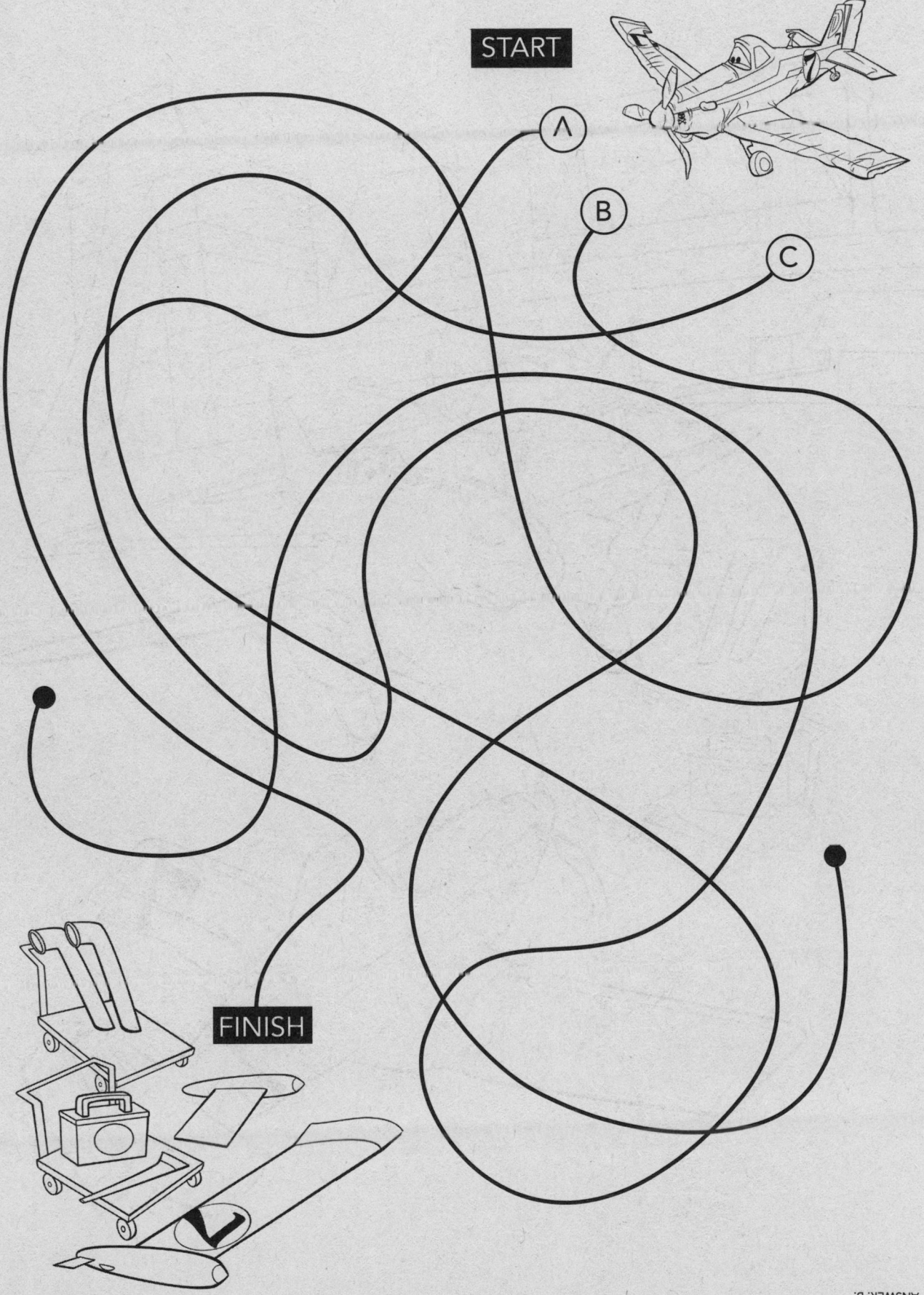

FINISH

Dusty's friends bring him new parts so he can be repaired.

Skipper finally admits to Dusty that he is afraid to fly.

A Mexican navy helicopter rescues him—but Dusty is too broken to fly.

Dusty flies too low and a giant wave crashes into him!

Dusty is caught in a storm!
Solve the maze and help him fly around the waves.

START

FINISH

In Mexico, El Chu and Bulldog watch the news and wait to hear about Dusty.

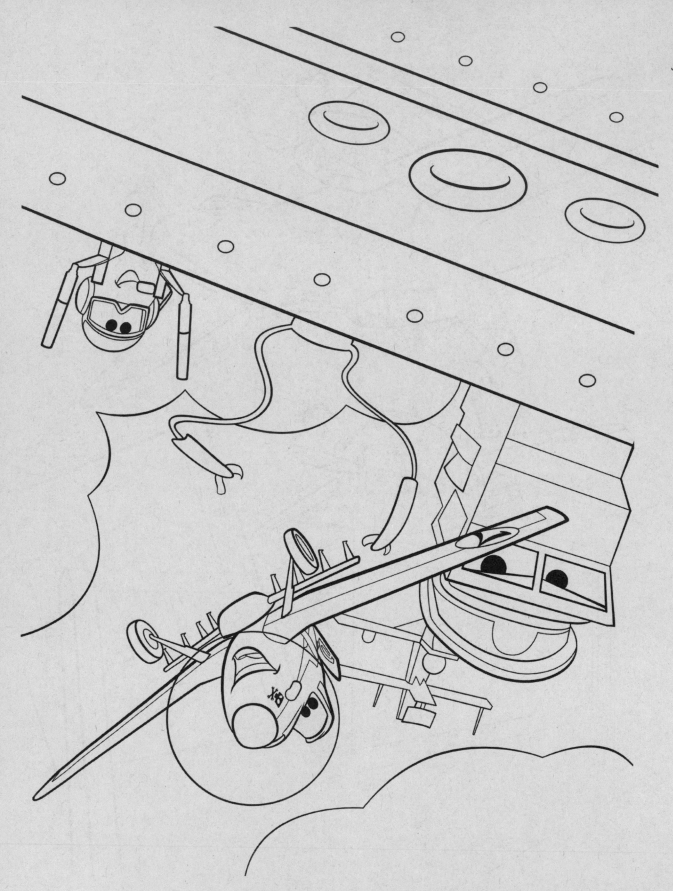

Whoo-hooo! Dusty launches off the USS Flysenhower and flies toward Mexico.

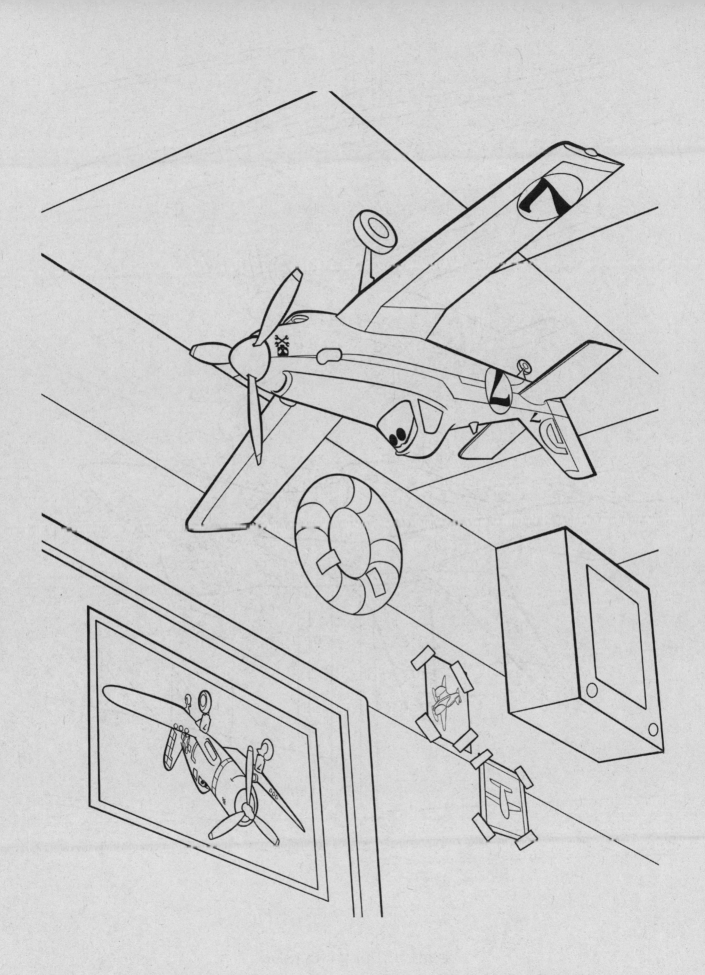

Dusty sees Skipper's picture on the Wall of Fame.

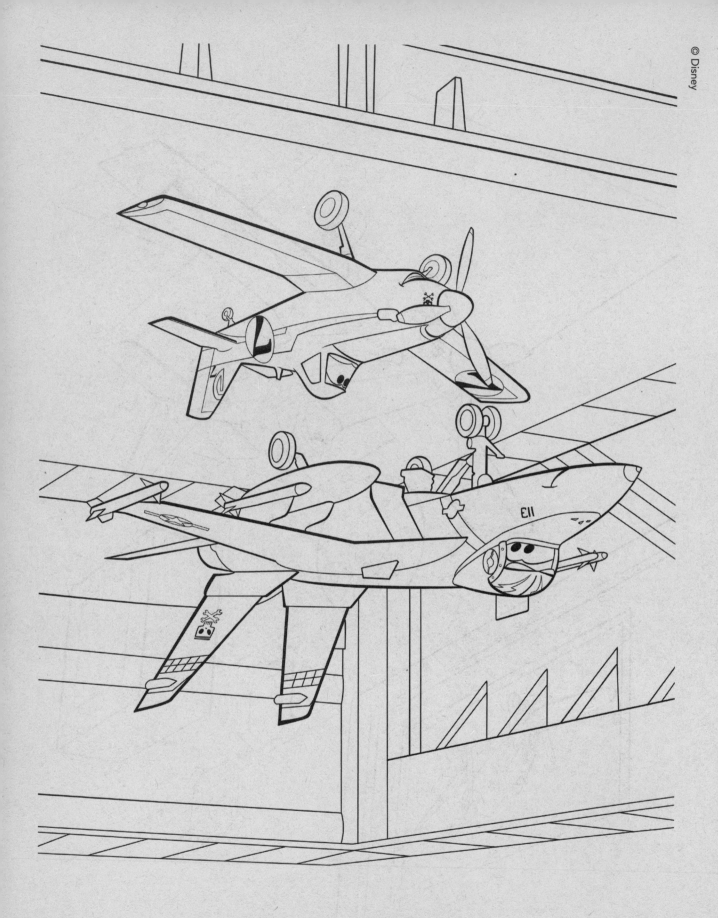

Echo takes Dusty to get repaired and refueled so he can get back in the race.

After the landing, everyone cheers for Dusty.
He even has fans on the USS Flysenhower!

With help from the fighter jets, Dusty bravely lands
on the aircraft carrier.

The captain gives the orders for Dusty to land.
Use the special code to find out the name
of the aircraft carrier.

S	F	E	N	Y	R	U	W	O	H	L
←	⬡	✳	△	✧	◉	☾	↑	✕	★	‖

___ ___ ___
☾ ← ←

___ ___ ___ ___ ___ ___ ___ ___ ___ ___ ___
⬡ ‖ ✧ ← ✳ △ ★ ✕ ↑ ✳ ◉

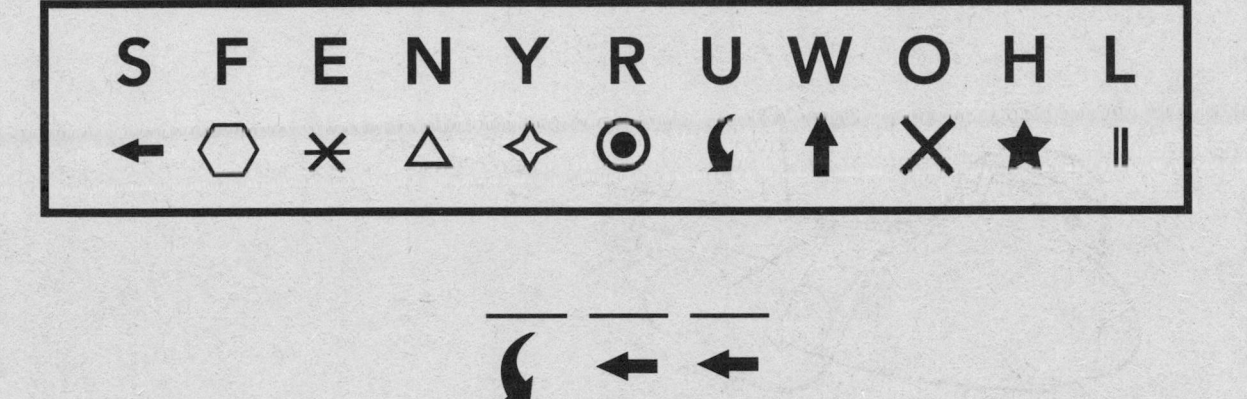

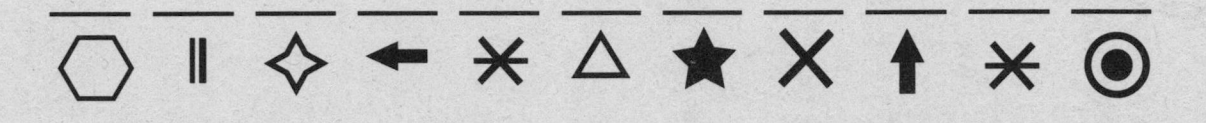

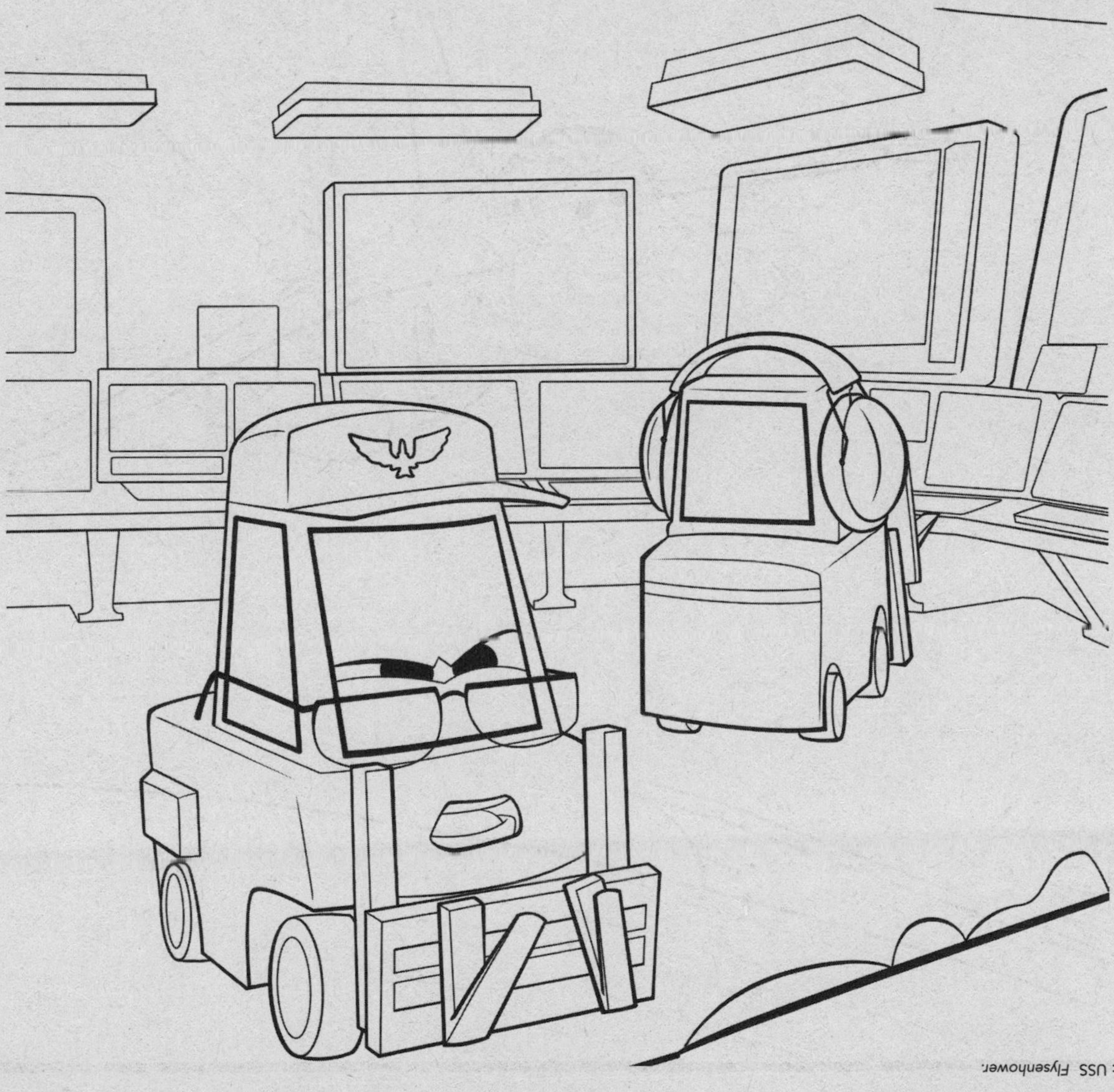

ANSWER: USS *Flysenhower.*

Color this poster to hang on your wall!

ANSWER: Echo and Bravo.

ROVBA
A _ _ _ _

HEOC
C _ _ _ _

Two navy jets guide Dusty to an aircraft carrier on the ocean.
Unscramble the letters to learn their names.

Dusty is almost out of fuel. A big fighter jet finds him just in time!

Without his radar antenna, Dusty becomes lost.

Oh, no! Dusty's antenna falls into the ocean! Who told Zed to break the antenna? Use the code below to find out.

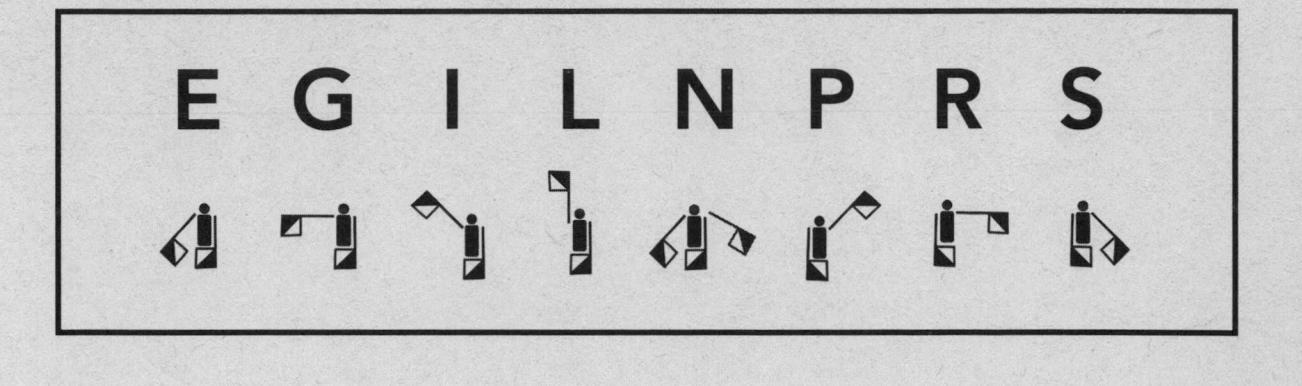

ANSWER: Ripslinger.

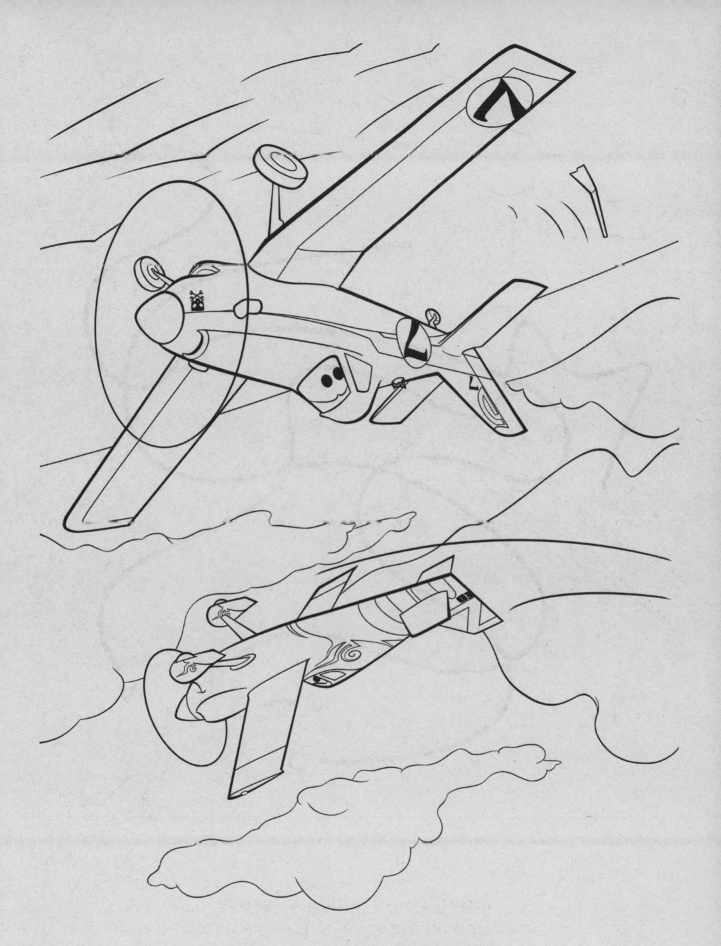

Zed breaks Dusty's antenna!
Now Dusty can't use his radio!

Ned and Zed are after Dusty!

Find the line that leads Dusty to the sun and away from the Twin Turbos.

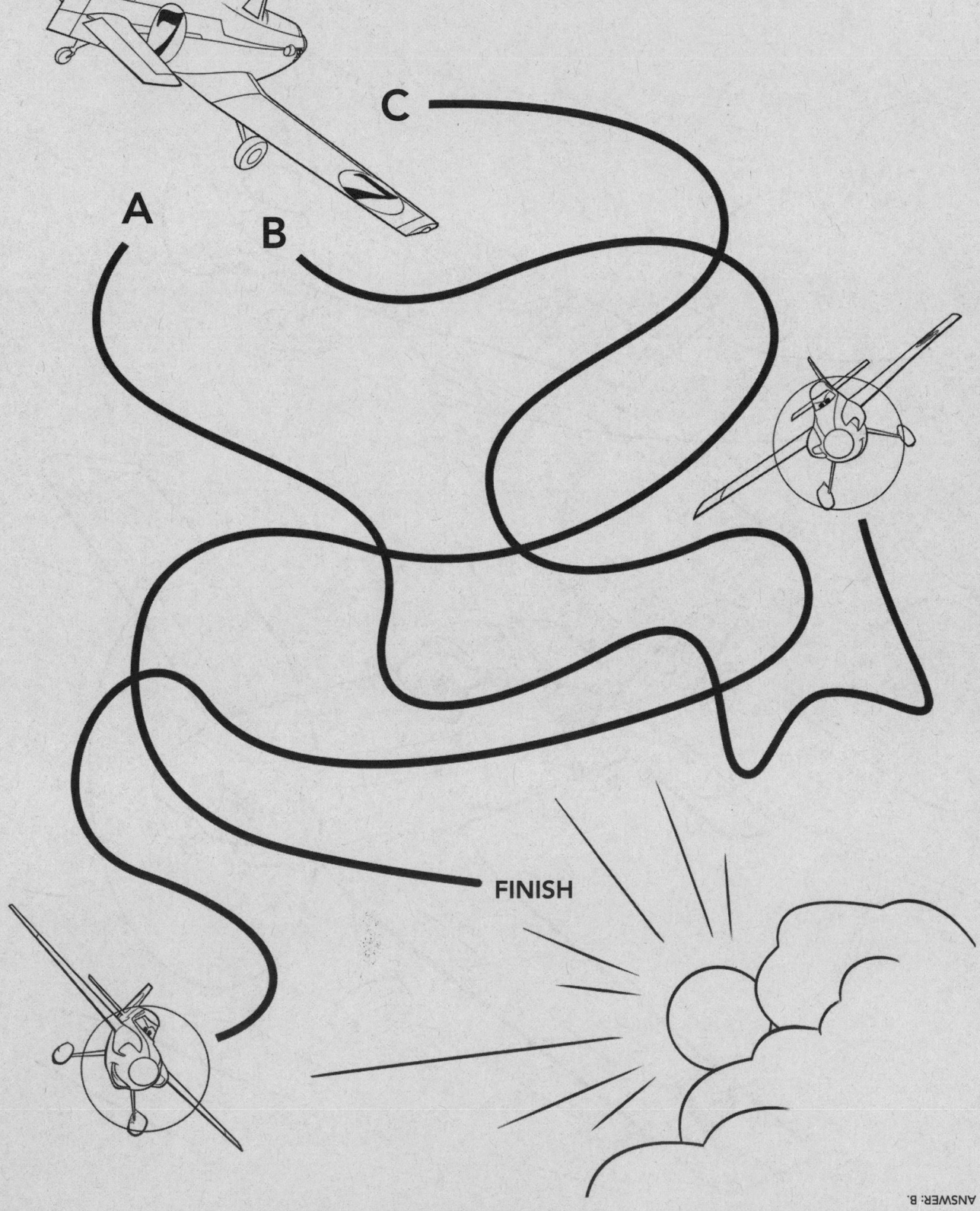

C

A

B

FINISH

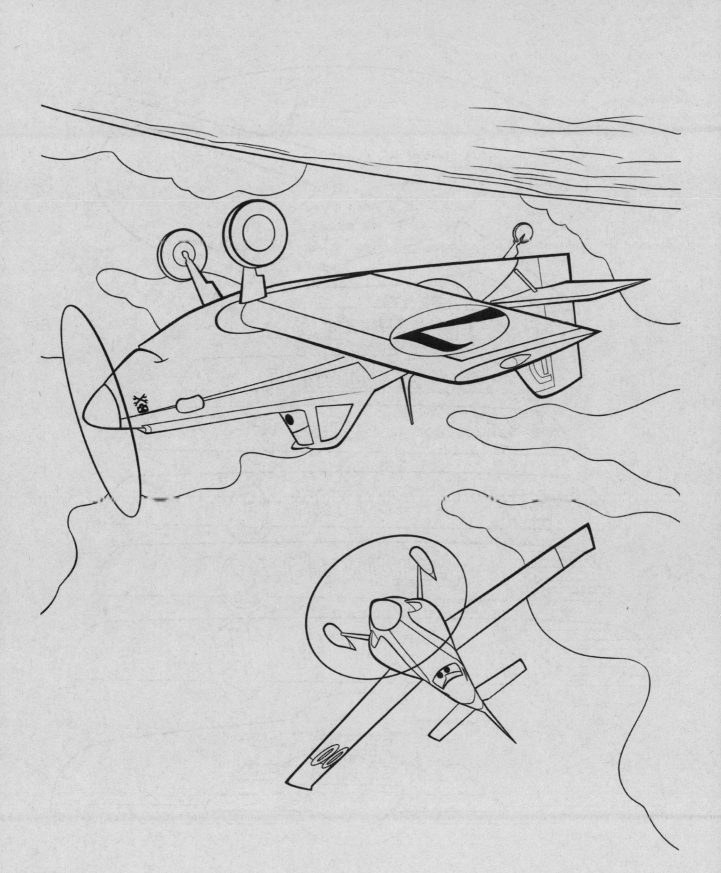

The race to Mexico begins, and Dusty flies low over the ocean.
He doesn't know that Zed is following him!

Dusty is in first place. Ripslinger wants to make sure that Dusty
loses the next leg of the race.

El Chu wins the heart of Rochelle when he sings her
a beautiful song.

Look at the top picture carefully. Then circle five things that are different in the bottom picture.

ANSWER:

Skipper, Chug, and Dottie have a surprise—they are going to Mexico
to join up with Dusty!

Back in Propwash Junction, Dottie and Chug
follow Dusty's race on TV.

Dusty lands in Nepal and finds out he's in first place!

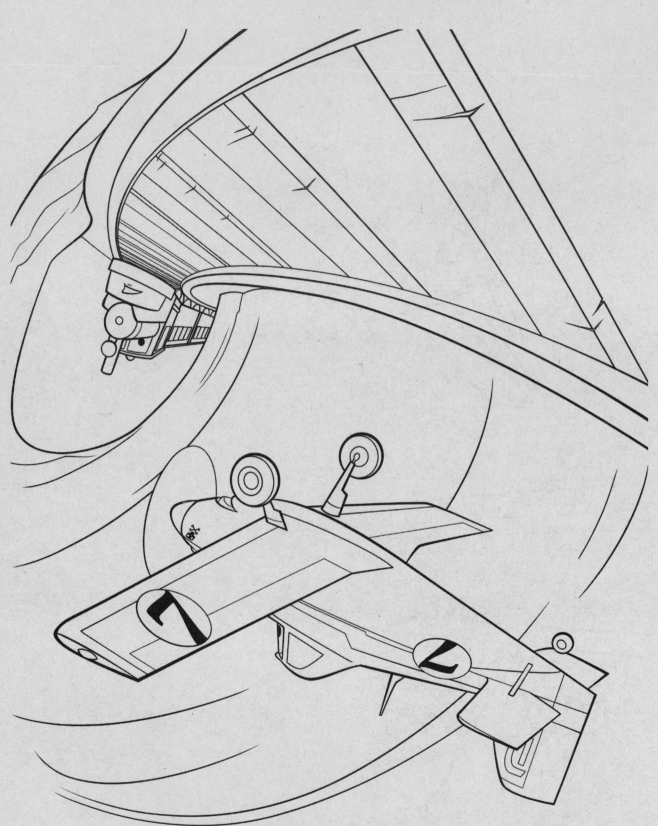

Dusty makes it through the train tunnel, narrowly
missing an oncoming train!

Dusty follows the railroad tracks through the mountains.
To find out the name of the mountains, begin at the letter *T*.
Then write every other letter in order on the blanks.

— — —

— — — — — — — — — —

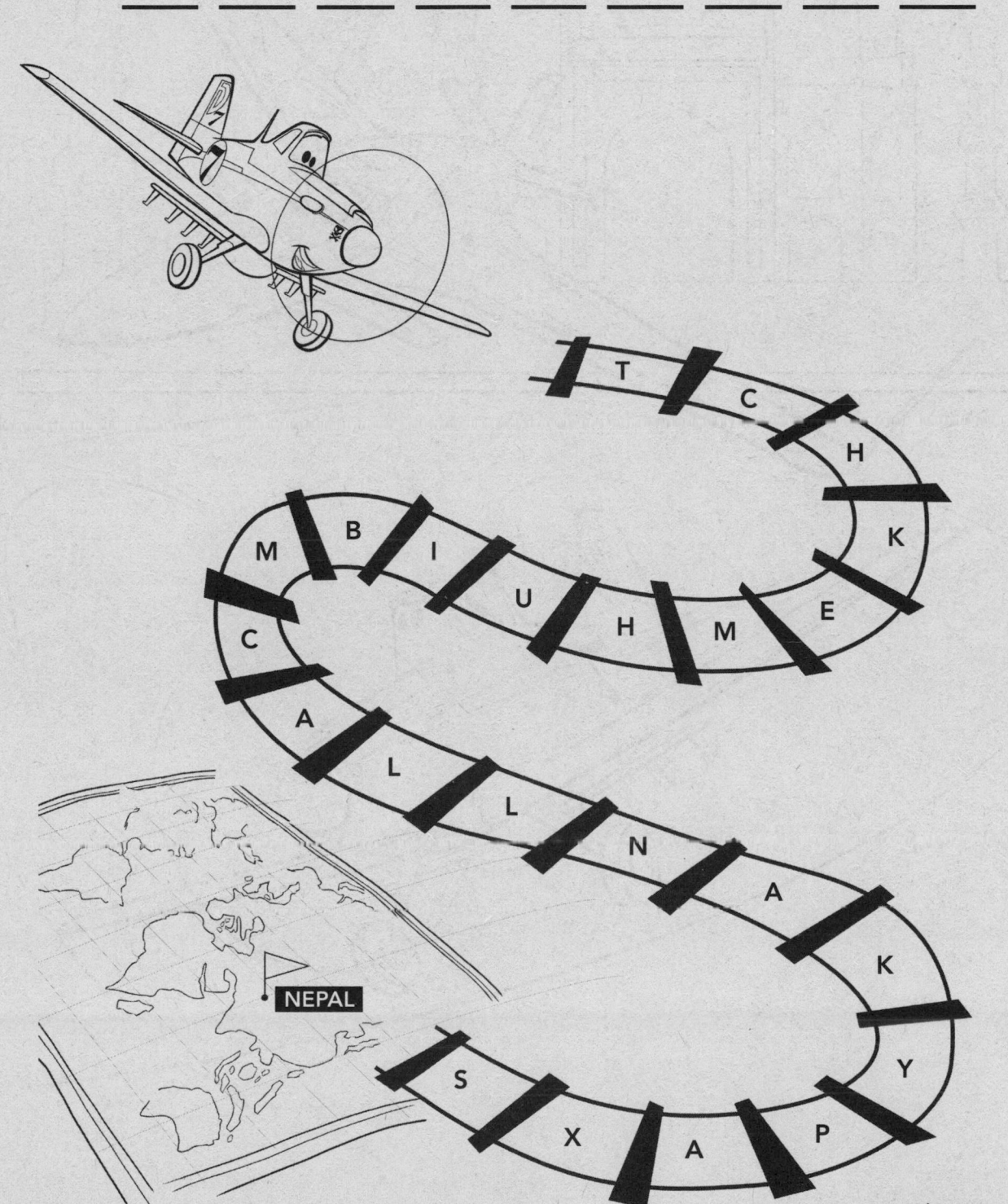

NEPAL

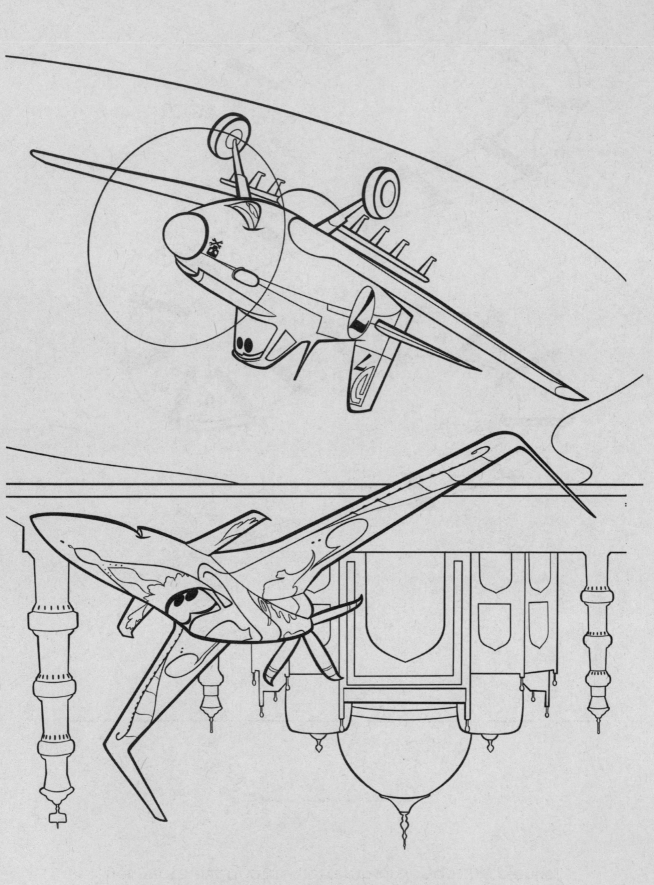

In India, Ishani shows Dusty the Taj Mahal and tells
him about a shortcut to Nepal.

Skipper tries to fly again, but he gives up before
he gets off the ground.

Dusty thinks Skipper is fearless.
He doesn't know that Skipper is afraid to fly.

Dusty tells the reporters that Skipper taught him how to race.

Dusty vs. Ripslinger!

With a friend, take turns connecting two dots below with a straight line. If the line you draw completes a box, put your initials in it and take another turn. Count two points for squares that contain Dusty and one point for each square with your initials. Subtract one point for squares with Ripslinger. When all of the dots have been connected, the player with more points wins.

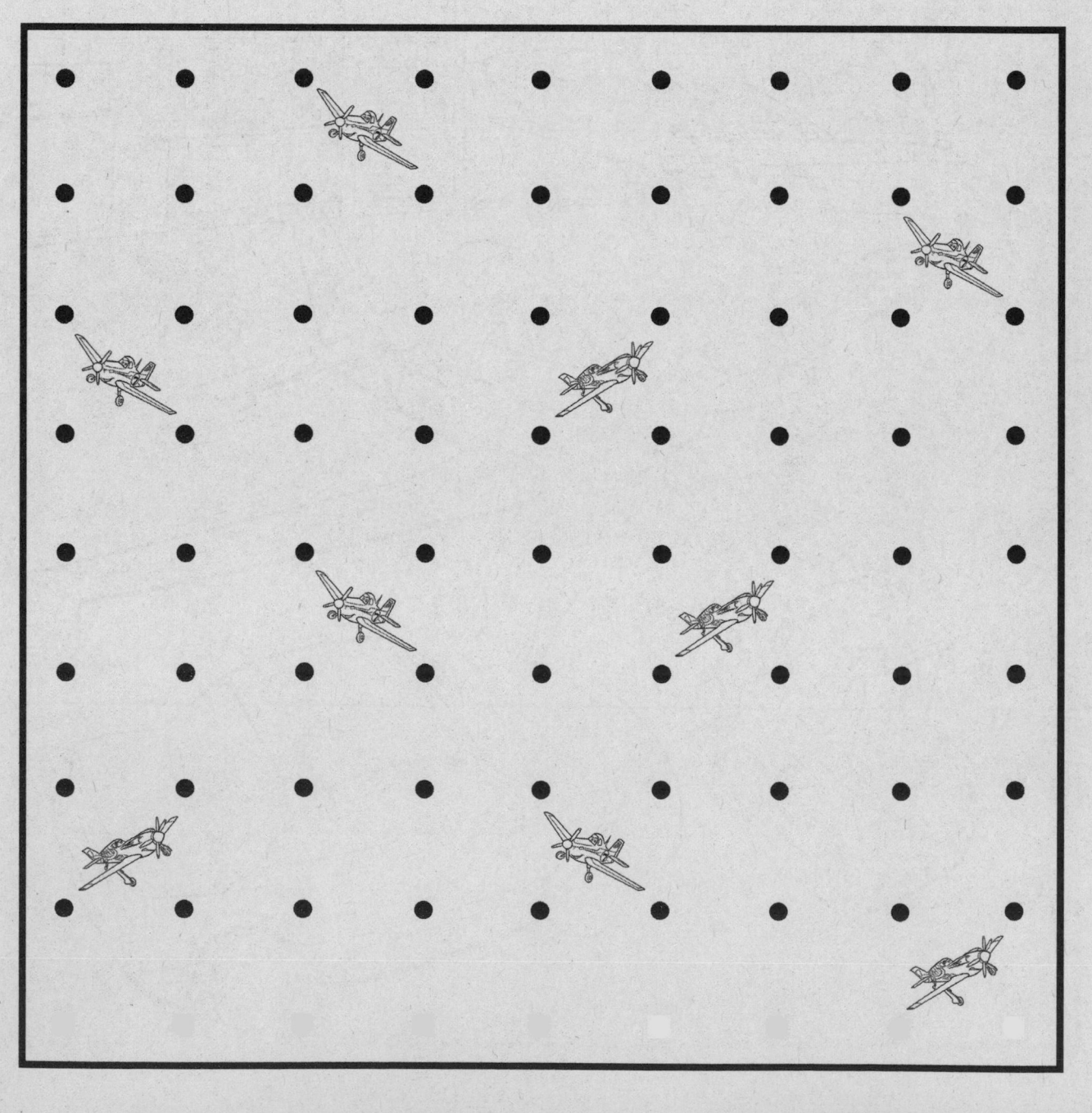

Dusty vs. Ripslinger!

With a friend, take turns connecting two dots below with a straight line. If the line you draw completes a box, put your initials in it and take another turn. Count two points for squares that contain Dusty and one point for each square with your initials. Subtract one point for squares with Ripslinger. When all of the dots have been connected, the player with more points wins.

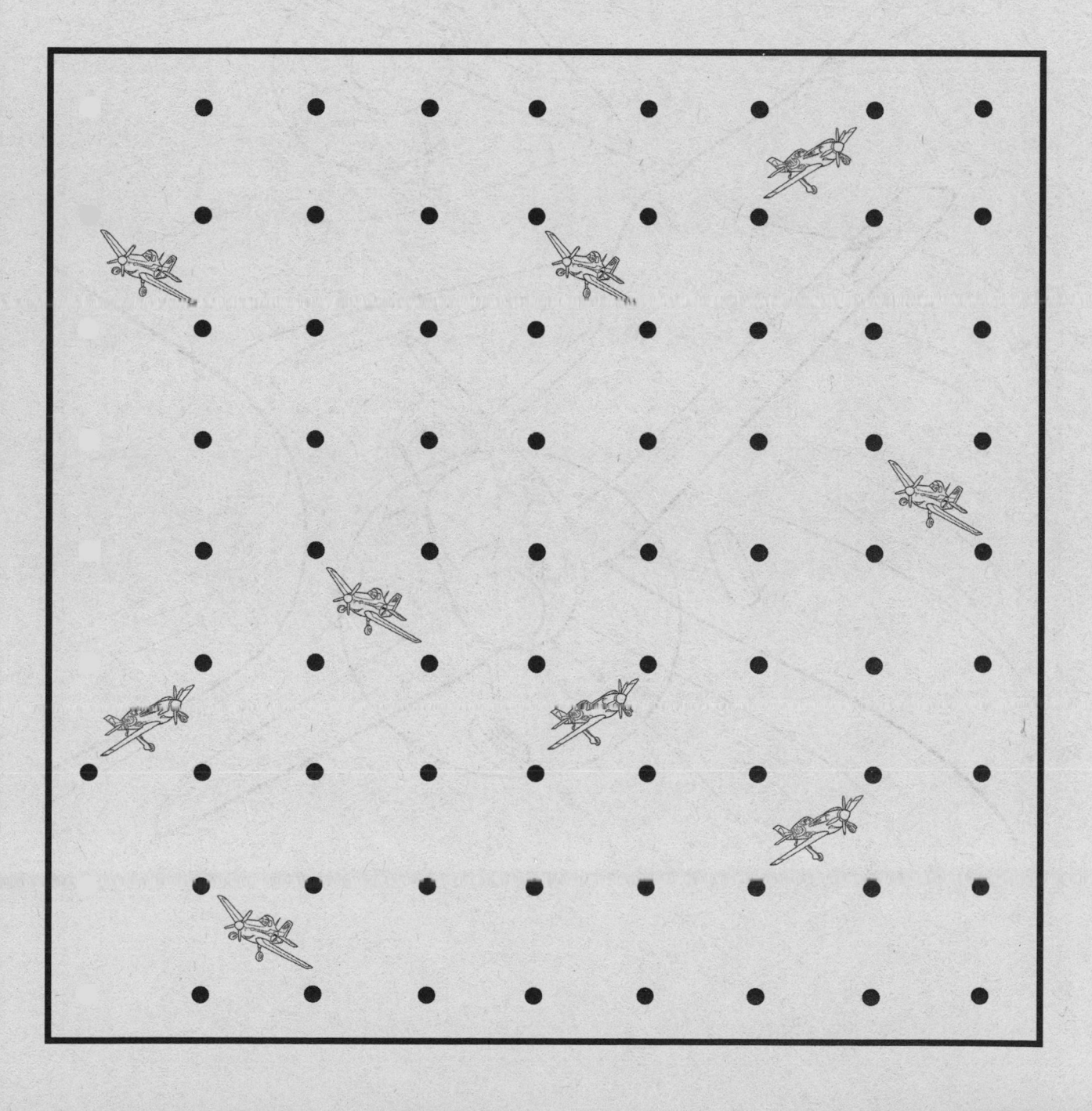

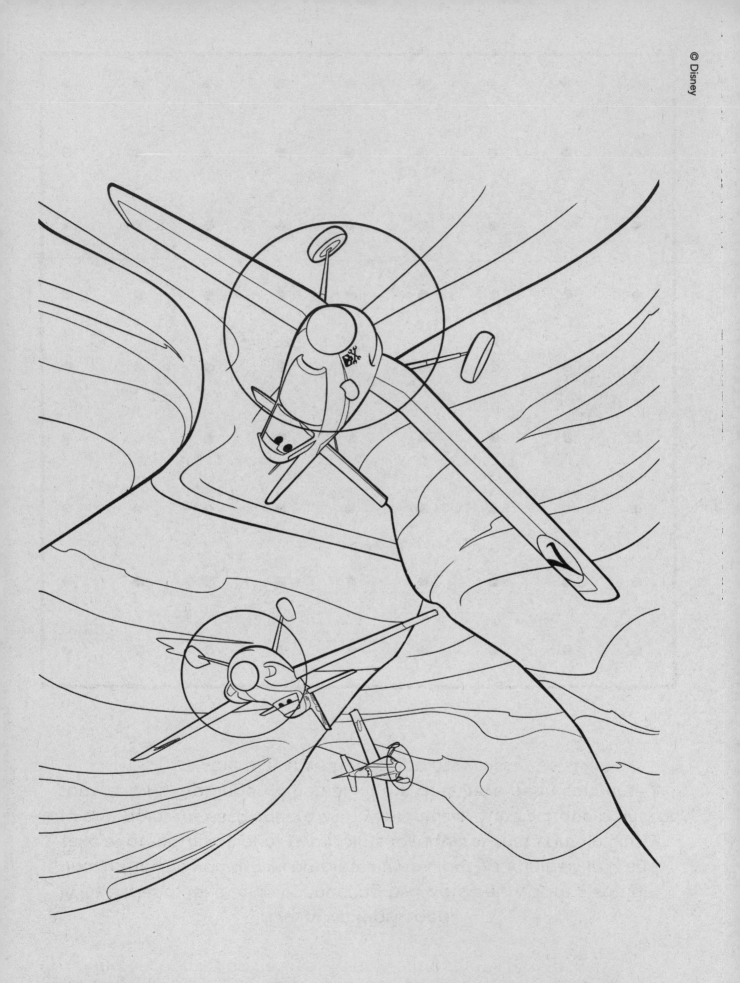

Flying fast and low, Dusty zooms through the mountains of India.

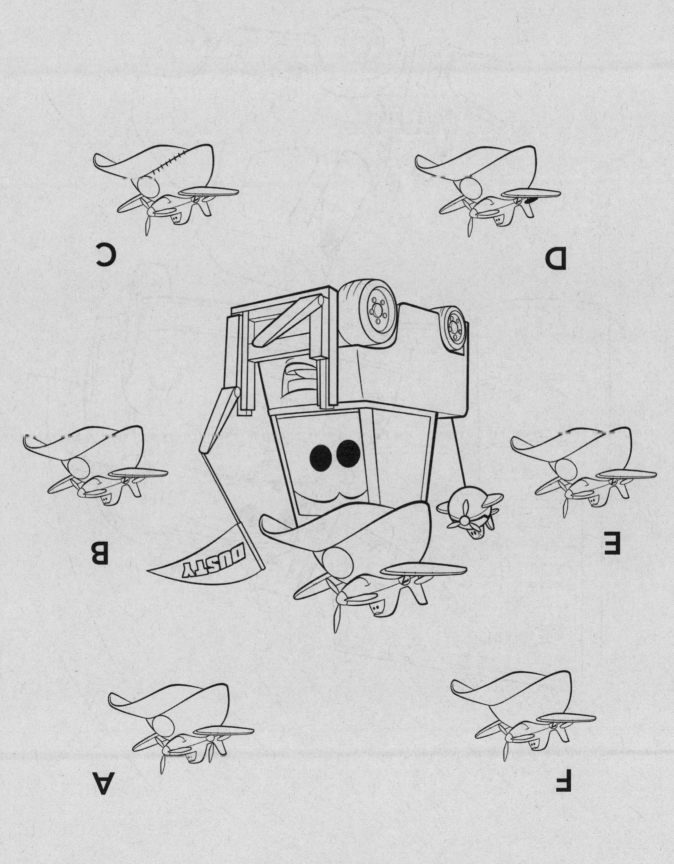

Sparky is a really big fan!
Find and circle the hat that matches the one Sparky is wearing.

Back in Propwash Junction, Chug and Dottie watch Dusty race on TV.

Dusty removes his sprayer so he can fly faster.

Use the code to learn his other name.

When Franz puts on his wings, he has a different name.

Dusty and El Chu meet a small German car named Franz.
He is a Flugzeugauto: a flying car!

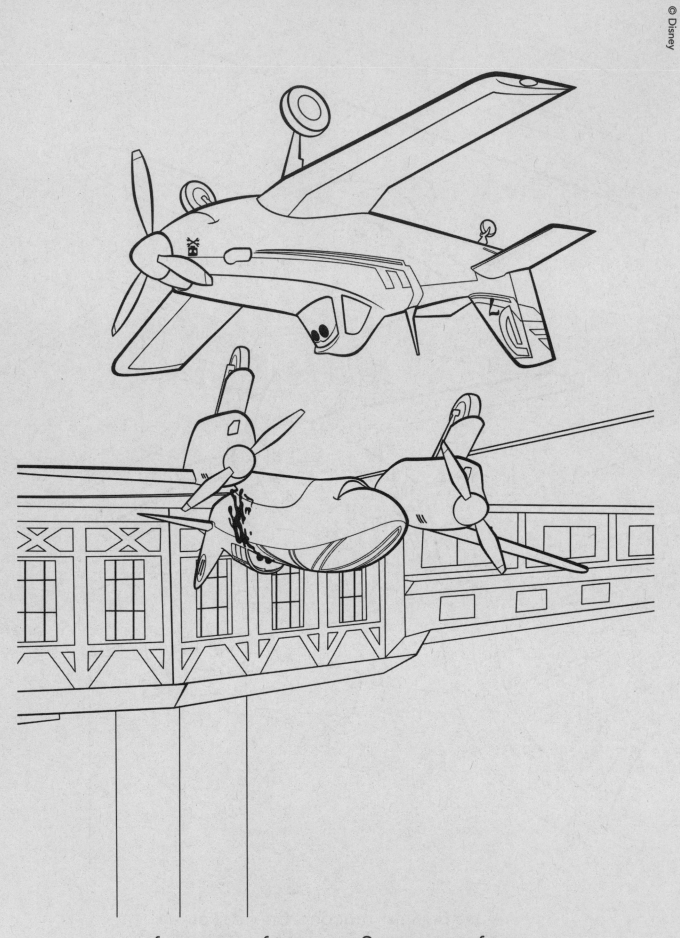

Dusty and Bulldog land safely in Germany.

Bulldog is leaking oil and can't see! But Dusty can help.
Find the line that leads Bulldog to Dusty.
Watch out for the trees!

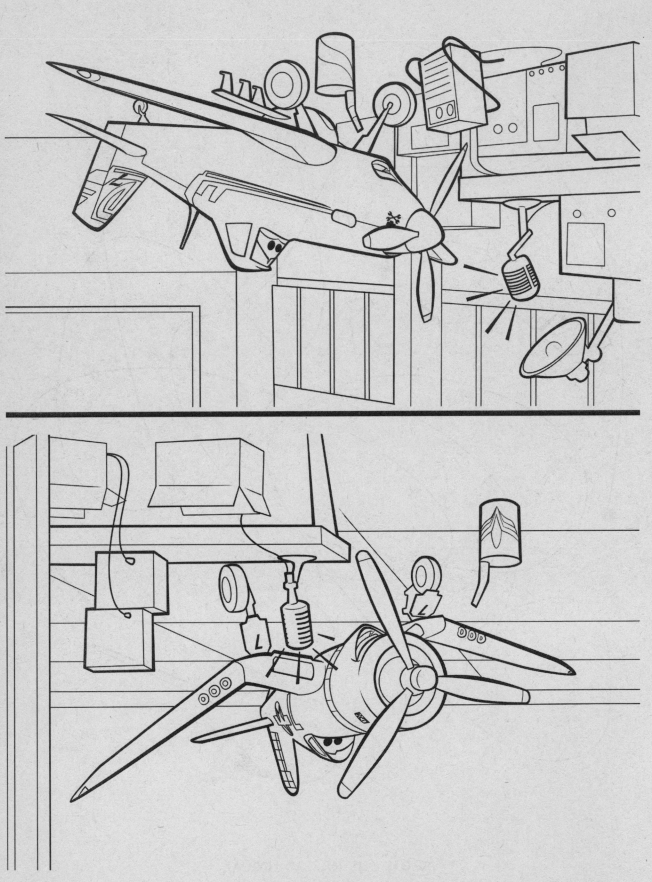

Skipper coaches Dusty over the radio. He wants Dusty to fly higher.

Dusty is caught in a storm!
Help him fly through the maze and land safely in Iceland.

START

FINISH

ICELAND

Dusty flies low, where the wind slows him down.

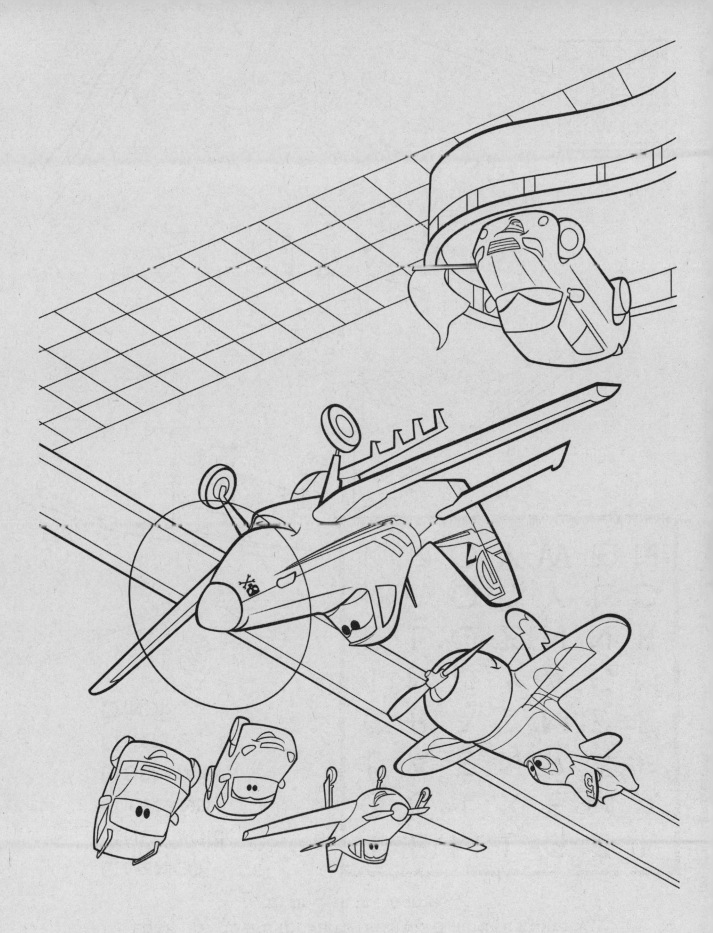

The Wings Around The Globe Rally begins! Dusty zooms into the air!

WINGS AROUND THE GLOBE MAP

Look up, down, forward, backward, and diagonally
to find all the names.

- ☐ MEXICO
- ☐ NEW YORK
- ☐ ICELAND
- ☐ GERMANY
- ☐ NEPAL
- ☐ INDIA

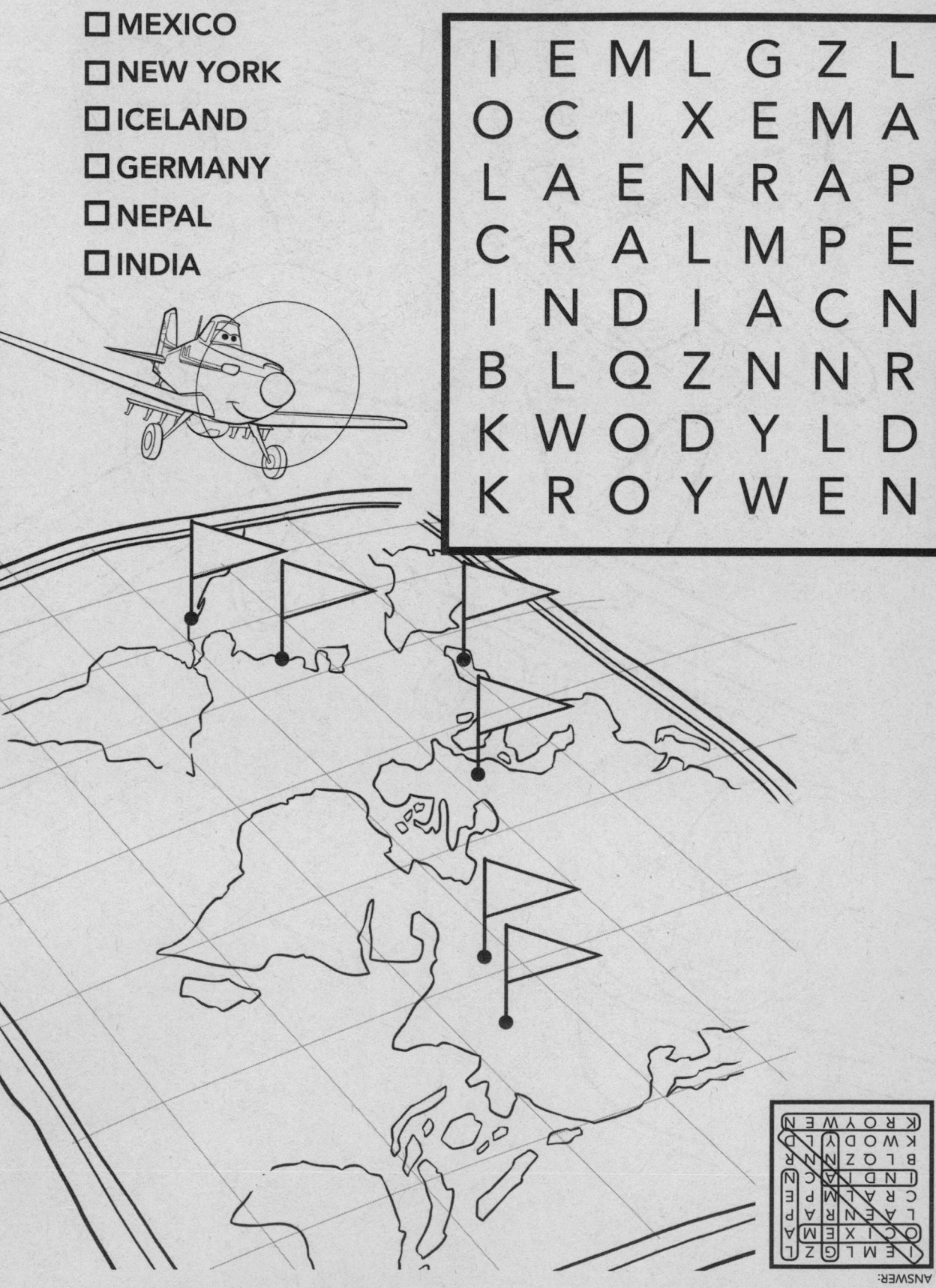

I	E	M	L	G	Z	L
O	C	I	X	E	M	A
L	A	E	N	R	A	P
C	R	A	L	M	P	E
I	N	D	I	A	C	N
B	L	Q	Z	N	N	R
K	W	O	D	Y	L	D
K	R	O	Y	W	E	N

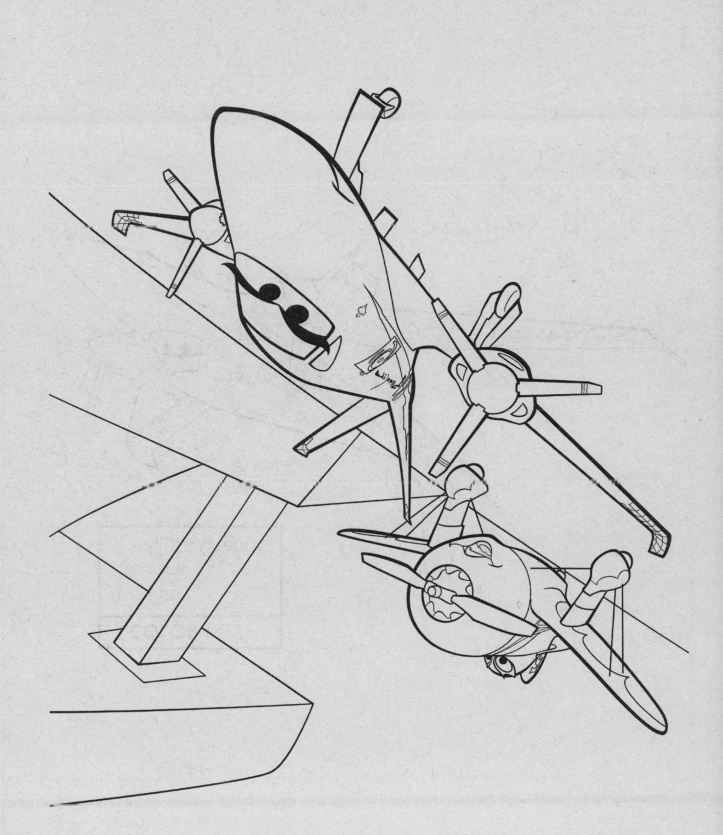

El Chu thinks Rochelle is beautiful.

Rochelle is a rally champion from Canada.
Use the key to color her.

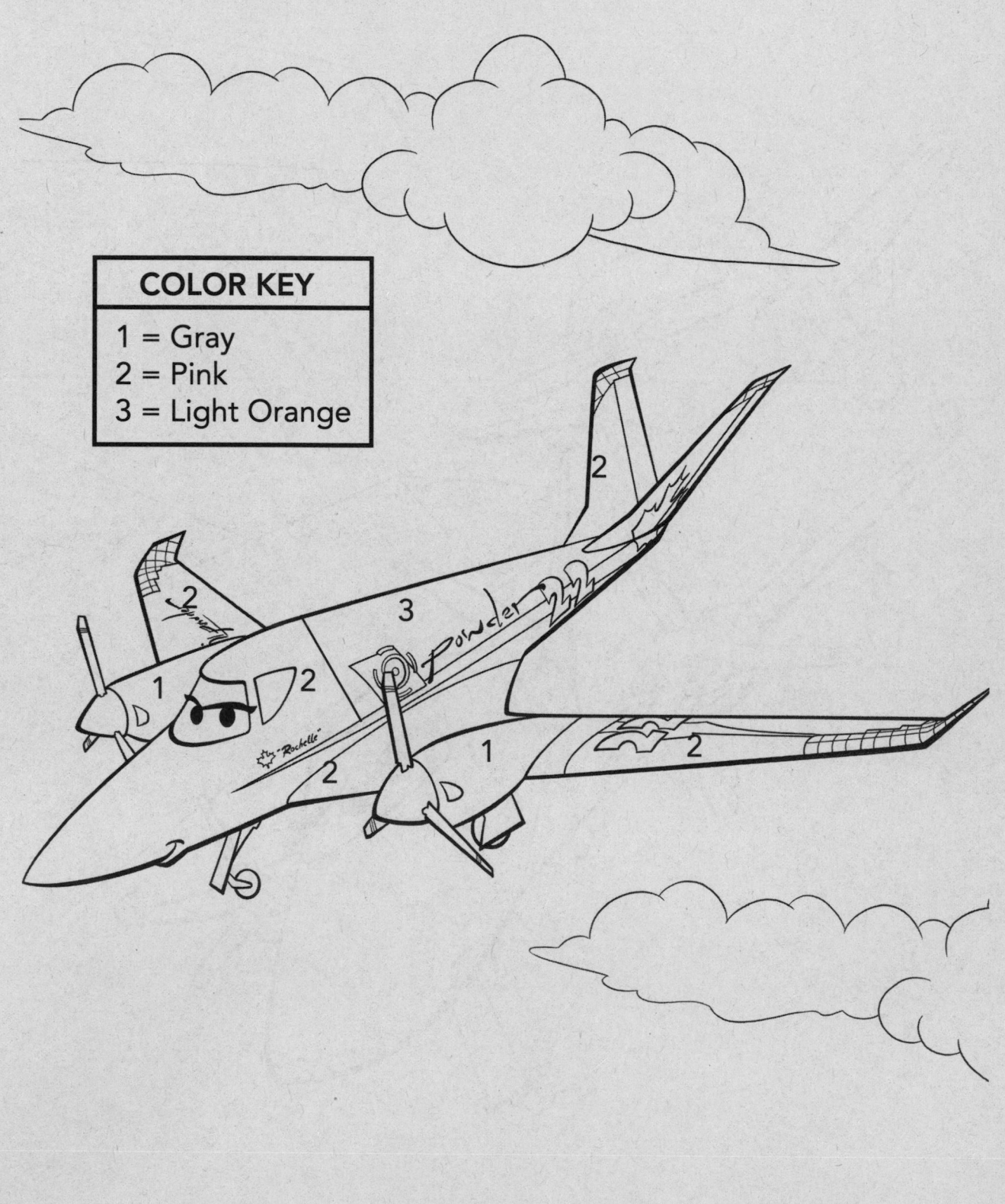

COLOR KEY

1 = Gray
2 = Pink
3 = Light Orange

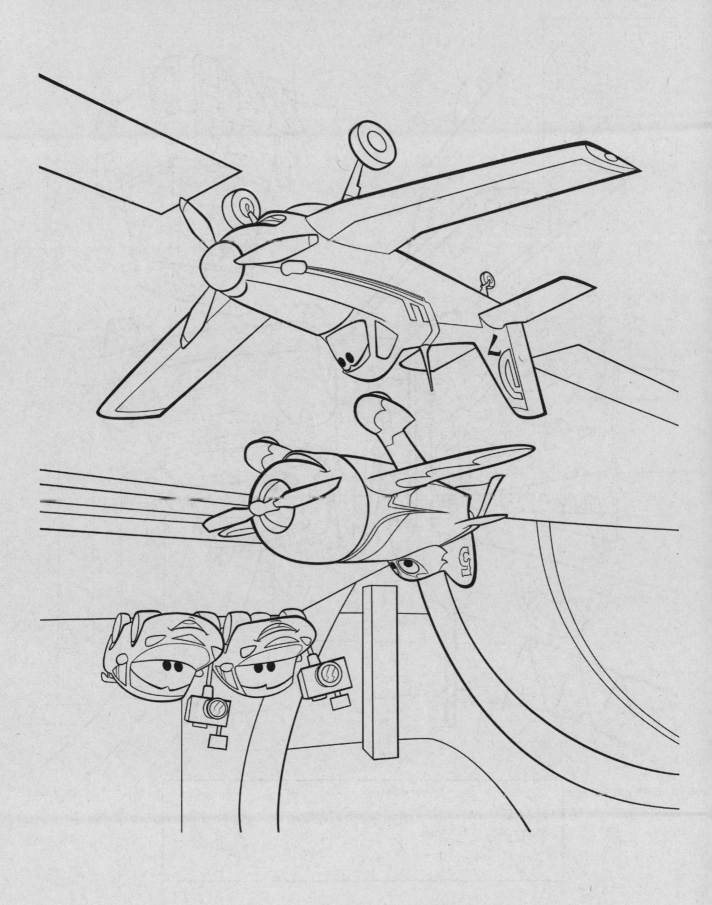

Dusty and his new friend El Chu head to the starting line.

ANSWER:

Dusty is lucky to have fans like Chug and Sparky.
Find and circle these four objects in the picture below.

The Racing Sports Network blimp has the best view of the racers.

© Disney

Color this poster of El Chu to hang on your wall!

Bulldog and El Chupacabra are very different.
They do not get along.

The racer from Mexico wears a cape and a mask. To learn his name, replace each letter with the one that comes before it in the alphabet.

FM DIVQBDBCSB

_ _ _ _ _ _ _ _ _ _ _ _

ANSWER: El Chupacabra.

BULLDOG

A

B

C

D

ISHANI

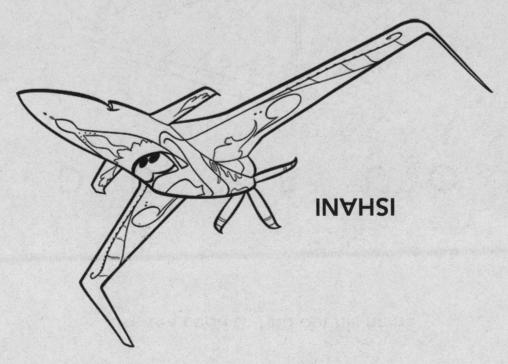

Draw a line from each close-up image to the plane it belongs to.

The racer from Great Britain is the winner of the European Cup.

Use the code to find out his name.

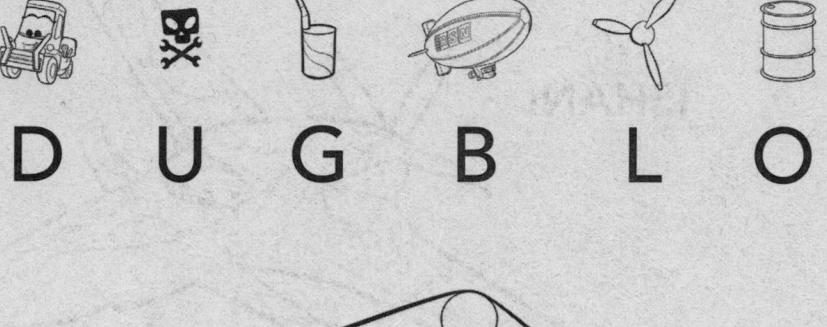

D U G B L O

_ _ _ _ _ _ _

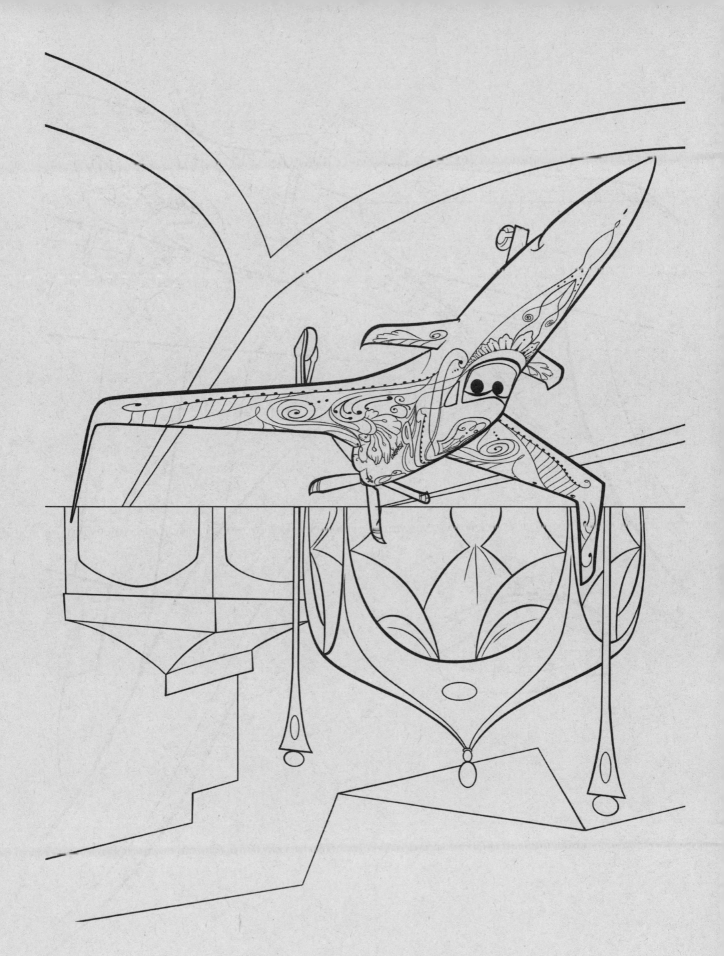

Ishani is a racer from India.

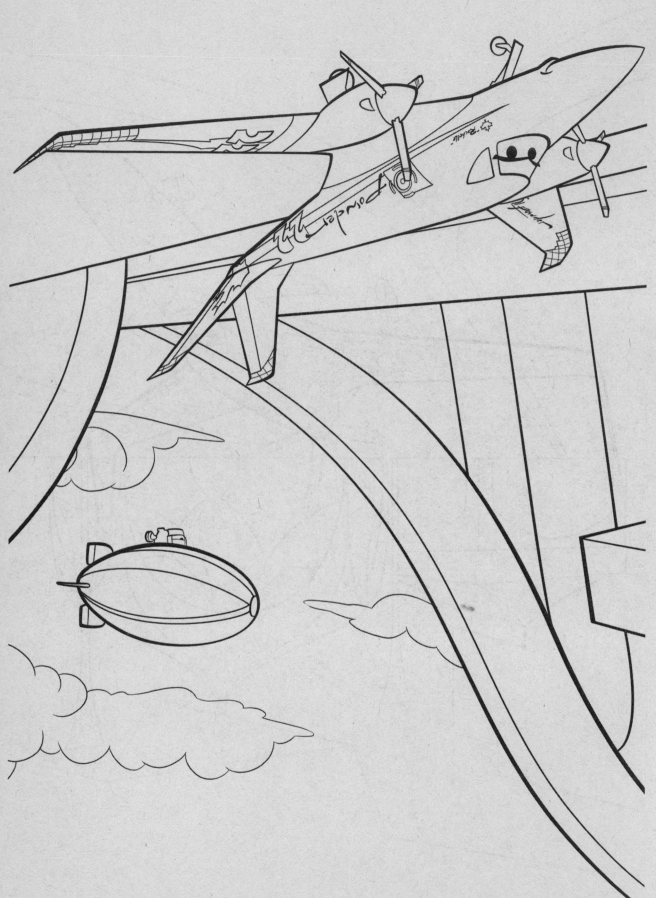

Rochelle is the Canadian Rally Rally champ.

Dusty meets the other racers at pit row in
the Wings Around The Globe Rally.

Solve the maze to help Dusty get to the rally.

START

FINISH

WELCOME RACERS

© Disney

Dusty and Skipper continue to train for the big race.

Solve the maze and help Dusty fly back to Skipper.

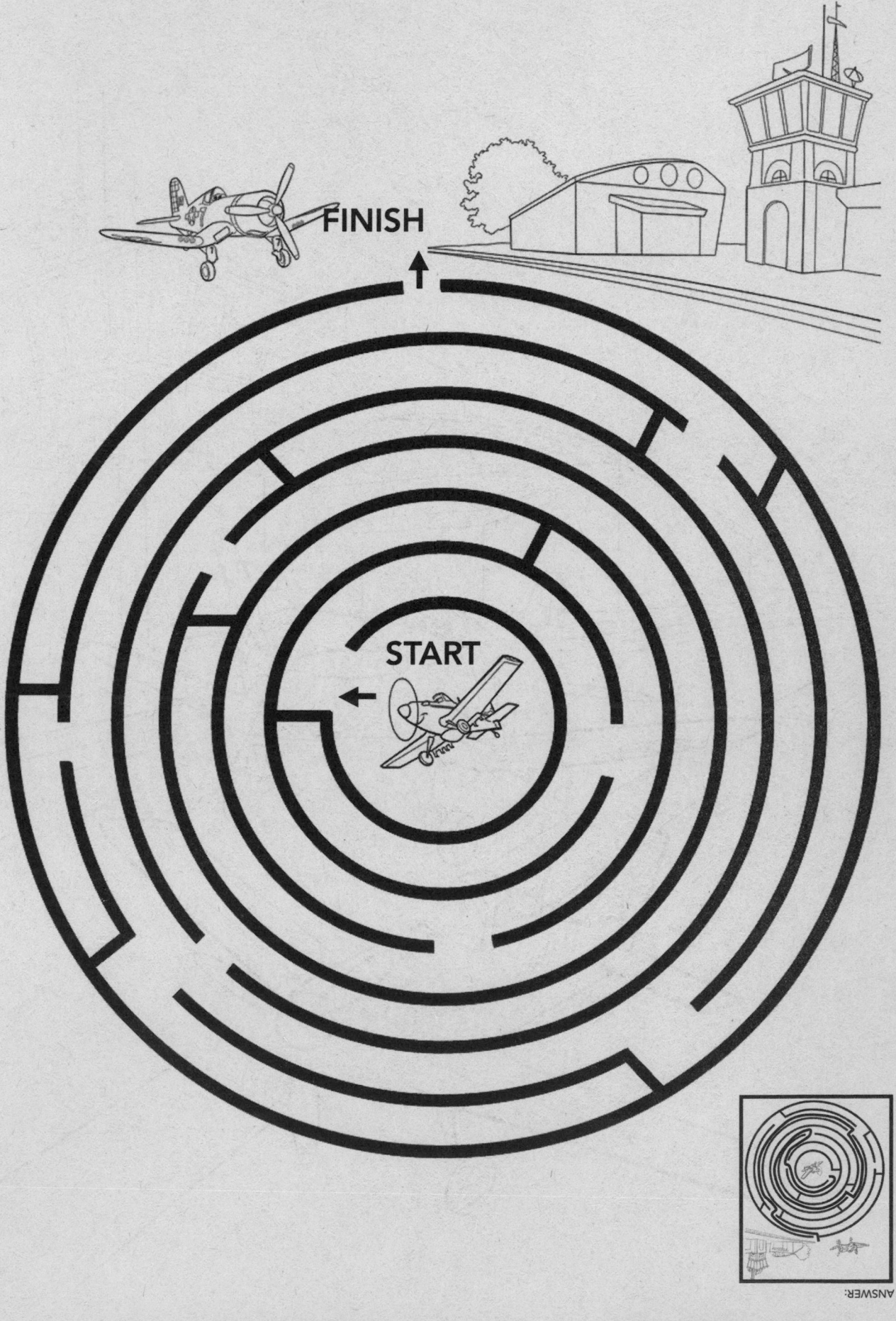

FINISH

START

ANSWER:

Skipper tells Dusty to fly up to the tailwinds, but the crop duster
is afraid of heights!

Skipper has Dusty race the shadow of a faster plane!

Skipper agrees to train Dusty, and they get ready for practice. Find and circle the five pylons hidden in the picture below.

ANSWER:

Chug tells everyone in town that Dusty is in the race!

When another racer drops out, Dusty is asked
to take his place!

Dusty returns to Propwash Junction and tries to forget about racing.

Dusty flew fast, but not fast enough to earn a spot in the race.

Zoom! Dusty flies across the finish line.

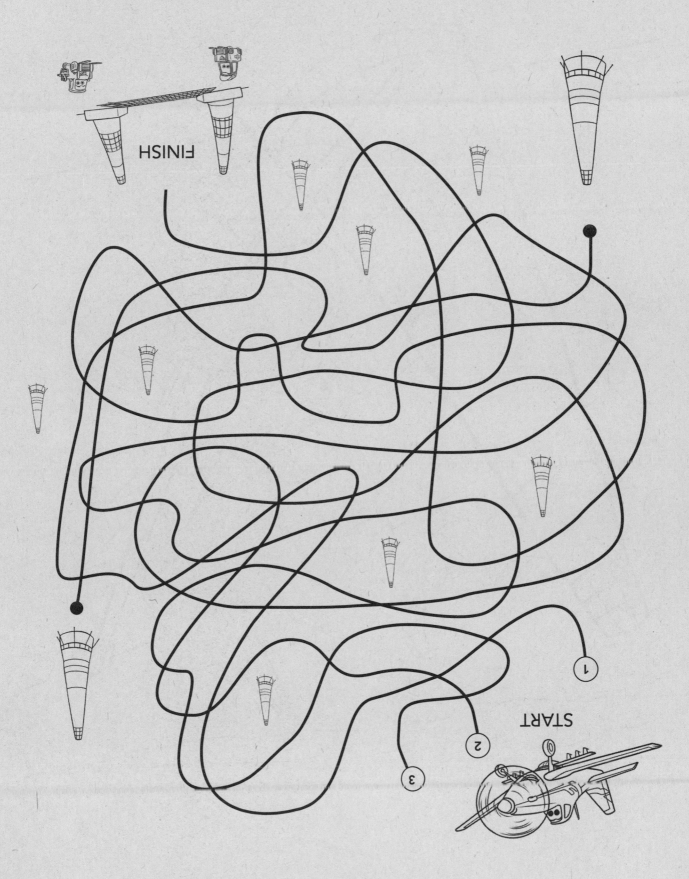

FINISH

START

1

2

3

Help Dusty find the fastest path to the finish line.
Watch out for the pylons!

Dusty flies faster than ever before!

It's Dusty's turn to fly. He rushes across the starting line.

Before the tryout begins, Chug and Dottie cheer Dusty on!

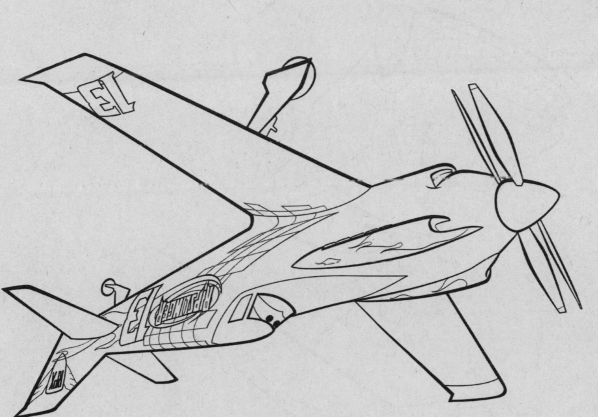

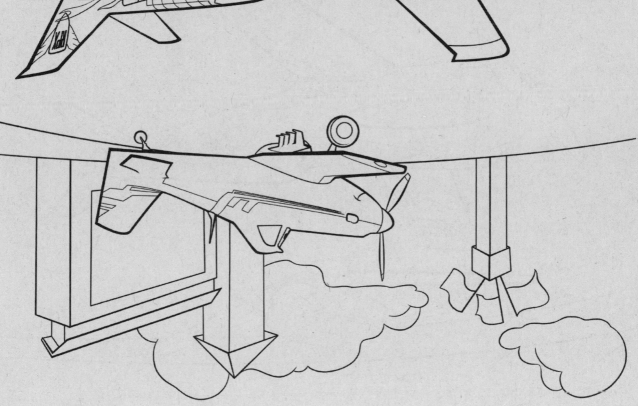

Ripslinger doesn't believe a crop duster like Dusty can fly in the race.

Dusty wants to meet Ripslinger, but Ripslinger is too busy talking to the press.

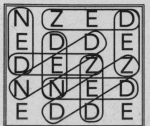

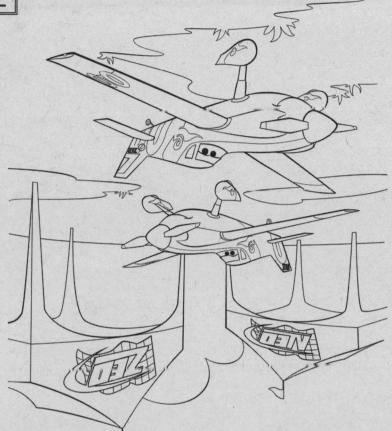

How many times can you find NED and ZED in the puzzle?
Look up, down, forward, backward, and diagonally.

Ned and Zed are twin turbo planes.

Circle the two pictures of Ned and Zed that are exactly the same.

A

B

C

D

E

Color this Ripslinger poster to hang on your wall!

To find out Ripslinger's nickname, go around the circle twice starting with the letter *T*, and write every other letter on the blanks below.

_ _ _ _ _ _ _ _ _ _

_ _ _ _ _ _ _ _ _

START

T
N   T
O   H
E   O
D   E
E   R
A   R   N   G

Ripslinger is the captain of team RPX.
Ned and Zed are his teammates.

ANSWER:

R	P	L	Z	N	E
E	I	T	T	O	D
P	D	S	G	H	C
P	O	U	N	P	H
I	T	H	S	D	U
K	C	U	R	T	G
S	P	A	R	K	Y

☐ CHUG

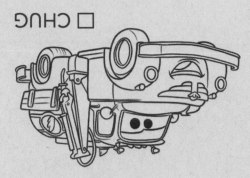

☐ DOTTIE

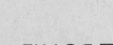

R	P	L	Z	N	E
E	I	T	T	O	D
P	D	S	G	H	C
P	O	U	N	P	H
I	T	H	S	D	U
K	C	U	R	T	G
S	P	A	R	K	Y

☐ SPARKY

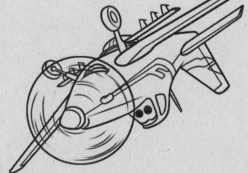

☐ DUSTY

☐ SKIPPER

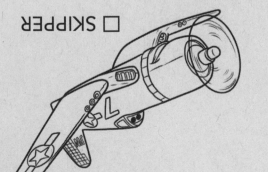

Look up, down, forward, backward, and diagonally to find all the names.

PROPWASH JUNCTION WORD FIND

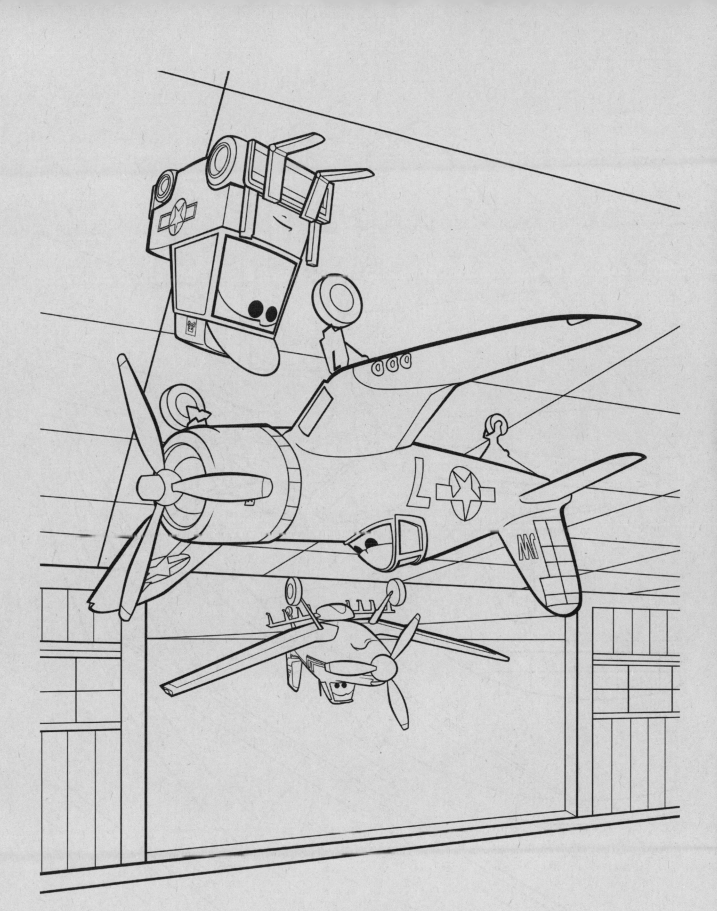

Skipper tells Dusty that he doesn't want to be his trainer.

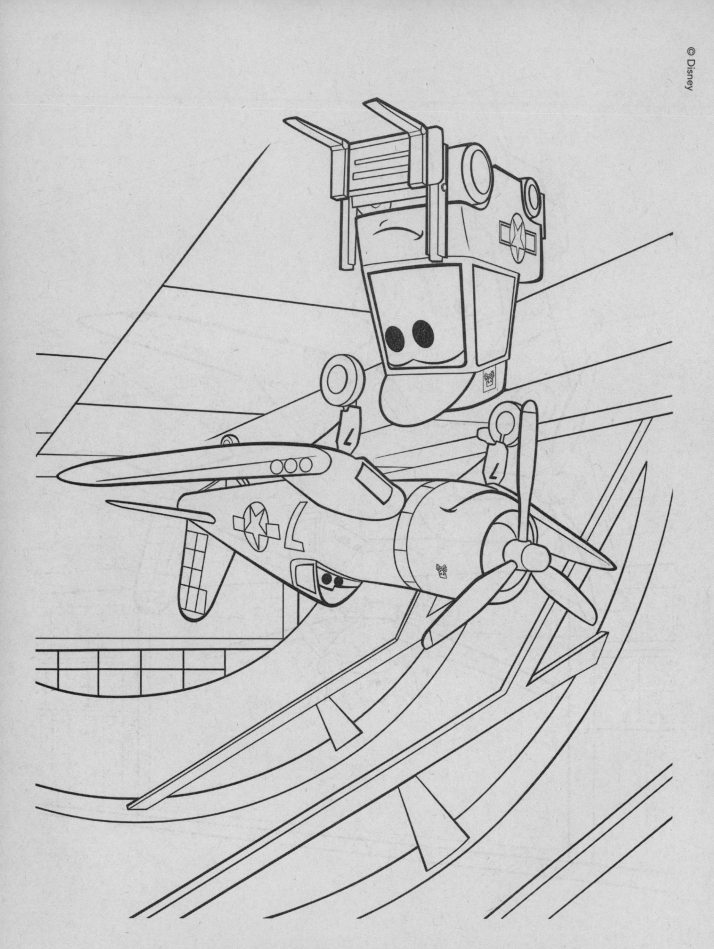

Skipper was a flight instructor, but he doesn't fly anymore.
Skipper's assistant, Sparky, helps him move around.

Chug takes Dusty to meet a plane that can help him train for the race.

Chug tells Dusty he needs a trainer with flying experience
for the Wings Around The Globe Rally.

A plane named Skipper uses binoculars to watch Dusty practice.

Circle four things that belong to Dottie.

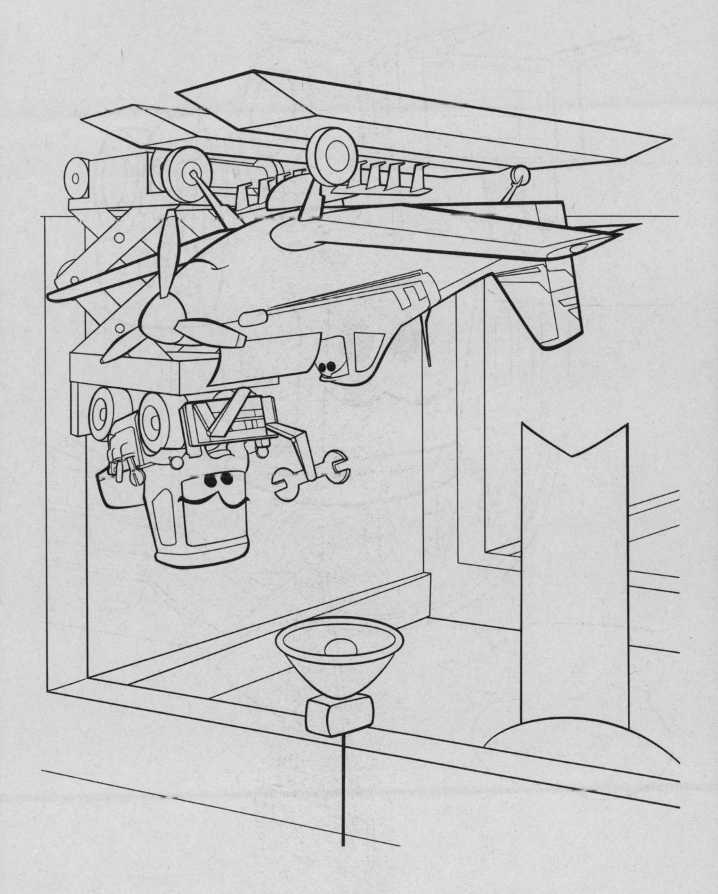

Dottie keeps Dusty in tip-top shape!

© Disney

Dottie is the best mechanic in Propwash Junction.

Solve the maze to help Dusty get through the obstacle course.

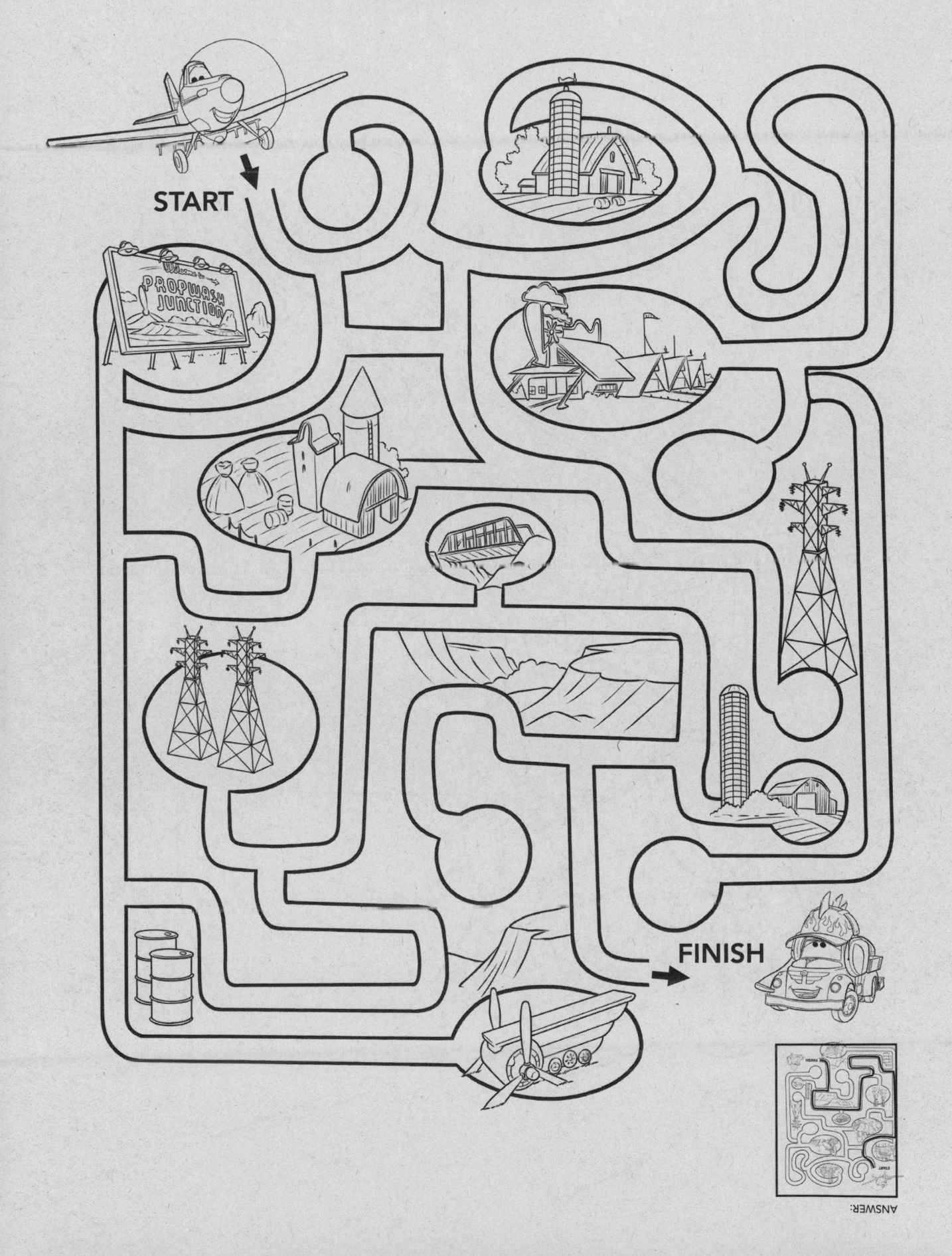

START

FINISH

Chug makes sure Dusty practices racing every day.

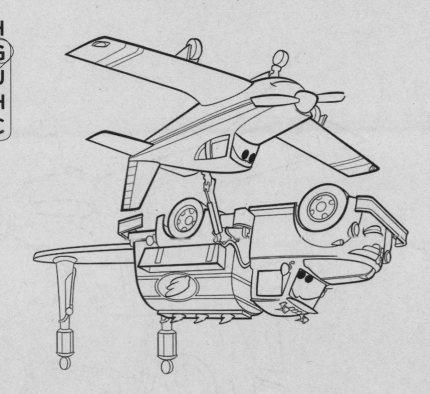

How many times can you find CHUG in the puzzle?

Chug makes sure the planes have plenty of fuel.

Dusty's best friend is a fuel truck named Chug.

Color this poster of Dusty to hang on your wall!

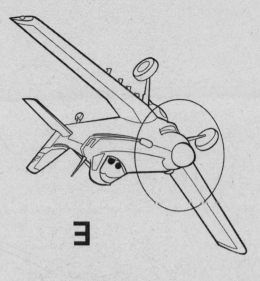

E

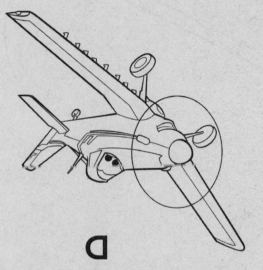

D

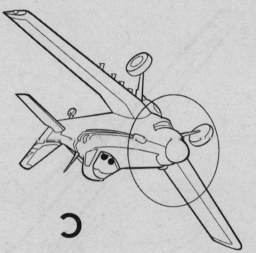

C

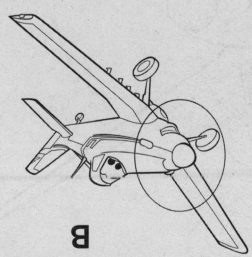

B

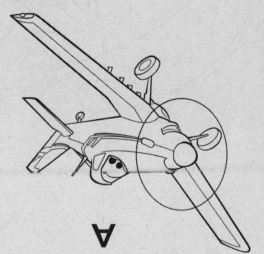

A

Circle the picture of Dusty that is different from the others.

Dusty dreams of becoming a racer.

Dusty Crophopper is a fast-flying crop duster from Propwash Junction.

Disney
PLANES

HIGH-FLYING FRIENDS

By Frank Berrios
Illustrated by the Disney Storybook Art Team

A GOLDEN BOOK • NEW YORK

Copyright © 2014 Disney Enterprises, Inc. All rights reserved. Published in the United States by Golden Books, an imprint of Random House Children's Books, a division of Random House LLC, 1745 Broadway, New York, NY 10019, and in Canada by Random House of Canada Limited, Toronto, Penguin Random House Companies, in conjunction with Disney Enterprises, Inc. Golden Books, A Golden Book, and the G colophon are registered trademarks of Random House LLC. Originally published by Golden Books in slightly different form as *Takeoff!* in 2013.

ISBN 978-0-7364-3231-3
randomhouse.com/kids
Printed in the United States of America
10 9 8 7 6 5 4 3 2 1